LOOSE ENDS

By

Michael A Greaves

LOOSE ENDS

ISBN: 9798398177954

LOOSE ENDS

This book is again dedicated to my wife Jan, my two sons Andrew and Mathew, and all my friends and family, some of whose names I have included in my fictitious story lines.

LOOSE ENDS

CONTENTS

*PROLOGUE*_____*11*

*Chapter 1*_____*15*
*Chapter 2*_____*21*
*Chapter 3*_____*26*
*Chapter 4*_____*30*
*Chapter 5*_____*32*
*Chapter 6*_____*34*
*Chapter 7*_____*39*
*Chapter 8*_____*45*
*Chapter 9*_____*51*
*Chapter 10*_____*57*
*Chapter 11*_____*59*
*Chapter 12*_____*63*
*Chapter 13*_____*70*
*Chapter 14*_____*78*
*Chapter 15*_____*84*
*Chapter 16*_____*86*
*Chapter 17*_____*90*
*Chapter 18*_____*95*
*Chapter 19*_____*102*
*Chapter 20*_____*109*
*Chapter 21*_____*115*
*Chapter 22*_____*118*
*Chapter 23*_____*123*
*Chapter 24*_____*131*

CONTENTS (continued)

Chapter 25_____139
Chapter 26_____145
Chapter 27_____149
Chapter 28_____156
Chapter 29_____161
Chapter 30_____166
Chapter 31_____172
Chapter 32_____177
Chapter 33_____183
Chapter 34_____191
Chapter 35_____197
Chapter 36_____203
Chapter 37_____208
Chapter 38_____211
Chapter 39_____214

EPILOGUE_____219

ABOUT THE AUTHOR_____229

I would like to thank my wife Jan for her continued support and encouragement, without which 'The Anglesey Mysteries' trilogy would not have been written. Also a big thank you to my son Mathew who again designed and produced the front cover of the novel, and my brother Geoff who was 'promoted' to Chief Proof Reader and Editor for 'Loose Ends'.

LOOSE ENDS

PROLOGUE

The text came while he was sat at his desk in the fourth storey rented offices of his sole practitioner law practice in the heart of the Dubai Financial District. The iPhone, which was one of his private phones and registered in the UAE, 'pinged' announcing the incoming call and the message icon appeared immediately in the window, showing that it had originated from an international, unknown caller. Jonathon reached across and, pressing the requisite keys, read the text within. It simply said "Contracts executed. Outstanding balance plus £15,000 expenses to usual account AB". The ex-pat solicitor smiled at the choice of words and immediately replied "Thank you, will do. Excellent service as usual. Will be in touch shortly to arrange further work of an investigative nature".

Details of the first of the two 'contracts' appeared two days later, firstly as a breaking story on the inside front page of the Manchester Evening News and then a day later, it was picked up by a couple of the national 'tabloids'. The second contract only made a couple of paragraphs on one of the inside pages a week later in the Yorkshire Evening Post.

The Manchester Evening Post had a main banner headline "Criminal Ex-Chief Superintendent of Police Serving Time in Strangeways Found Hanged in his Prison Cell". There was then a half page story recapping his case and the circumstances of his death, which were given as suspected suicide by hanging. The national tabloids ran with the same storyline plus more background, but the same conclusions, pending further enquiries by the Prison Service and Home Office. It had been bad enough publicity for the Police at the time, that a high-ranking, serving officer had been found guilty of involvement in gemstone smuggling, prestige car theft and money laundering amongst other offences. But now also to be found hanging in his cell was giving the tabloids and social media open season on the Police, whilst also resurrecting the periodically often run story of accusations of systemic corruption within the Force.

The Yorkshire Evening Post had a much briefer story regarding the second contract, and simply reported that two brothers serving life at the maximum-security prison in Wakefield had died, following a serious altercation between the siblings involving homemade knives: one of the brothers dying in the fight in the exercise yard and the second brother the following day from his injuries. The authorities confirmed in an official statement that they were unaware of any reason for the fight.

With an air of quiet satisfaction and full retribution fully served, Jonathon returned to the contract he was drawing up on behalf of his new employer, a distant cousin of the head of the Dubai Royal Family. It was a position he had successfully applied for and got with the help of his good friend and business associate, Andre Botha, who himself had been previously employed in the Sheik's personal security division.

LOOSE ENDS

LOOSE ENDS

Chapter 1

A couple of weeks after the news of ex-Chief Superintendent Jonny Radcliffe's apparent suicide in his cell at Strangeways Prison in Manchester had broken, the man who had led the main investigation into his and his co-conspirators' alleged illegal activities, Chief Superintendent Geoff Washbourne, called a meeting of the case's main investigative five-man team at New Scotland Yard. The team under Washbourne consisted of Detective Inspector Richard Greenwood, Detective Sergeant Foden, Detective Sergeant Booth, Detective Constable Stones and Detective Constable Bell.

"Good morning gentlemen," the Chief Superintendent opened the meeting promptly at 8:30am, after the five detectives had helped themselves to a coffee and some biscuits from a side table, and then arranged themselves around the oval conference table facing their senior officer. "After almost two years of absolutely no intelligence garnered from our ongoing search for the very elusive Jonathon T Underwood, and the missing millions from his alleged illegal activities, we are at last in the possession of a very interesting development, albeit from the pages of a couple of our more lurid tabloids. I presume you are all familiar with the details of Jonny Radcliffe's headline grabbing demise?" Washbourne asked, looking for confirmation from the detectives sat facing him, who all nodded silently. "We all know that our Mr Underwood is an exceedingly intelligent and very careful man, but that he is also totally ruthless. I think we can safely assume that Radcliffe's death was not, as the Home Office would like us to believe, suicide and that Underwood has decided, as we had always anticipated he would, after quite a lengthy period of inactivity, to right what must appear to be in his eyes, several wrongs that have been perpetrated against his good self and his criminal associates. Namely, his betrayal by Radcliffe and probably, in fact almost certainly, an attempt to recover the large amount of money, or at least what is left of it, that Radcliffe and his mysterious partner diverted from the criminal group's offshore accounts. In other words, gentlemen, I believe that our Mr Underwood has finally decided it is about time to tie up a few loose ends. Any questions at this stage?" Washbourne asked again looking round the table.

"No Sir," Detective Inspector Greenwood answered for his team.

"Okay Richard, I think a general update from you and your team, as to what we do and don't know at this point would be useful, especially for me," the Chief Superintendent continued.

"Unfortunately, Sir, as you are aware, it is mostly what we still don't know. On the plus side, we successfully gained convictions for Underwood's main partners Radcliffe and Williams, who are still locked up – well, Radcliffe was until last week," Greenwood smiled before continuing. "We also broke up the gemstone smuggling and car theft rings, including several convictions, but those people are not directly connected with Underwood, so I think we can discount them. We have been monitoring all the accountant Williams's visitors, and any other possible contacts, plus his wife Abigail's, but have turned up absolutely nothing to give us a clue as to Underwood's whereabouts; if he has somehow contacted them, how he eluded us, or what happened to him after we rounded up his fellow conspirators. We presume he must have had help, and no doubt is still receiving it, but we have no idea from where or from whom. The other big unanswered questions are what happened to all the money, and of course the identity of our mystery IT man, Radcliffe's colleague who handled all the money transfers to and from the offshore accounts, and ultimately relieved his fellow criminals of their hard-earned cash. We still have no idea who he is, where he is or where the money is."

"Exactly gentlemen," the Chief Superintendent said on the conclusion of Greenwood's report. "I am sure that Underwood took Radcliffe's betrayal and the loss of his ill-gotten gains very personally, knowing what we do about the solicitor. So, I think Radcliffe's death is the first step in his retribution, and we know that with his contacts within the criminal fraternity, Underwood would have had no problem paying for someone to arrange Radcliffe's death, on this occasion by an apparent 'suicide' in Strangeways. This is something we are pretty sure he has done at least once before. I am referring, of course, to the deaths of the three Irish people over at the farmhouse in Larne, who we believe stole a consignment of his smuggled gemstones. If my guess is correct, and at the moment that is all it is, until we have some kind of evidence to confirm Underwood's intentions, then it is up to us to stop him extracting any further retribution and find this mystery IT man before the solicitor does, and an added bonus of course, would be to retrieve whatever remains of the proceeds of their criminal activities."

After a brief pause the silence was broken by DI Greenwood.

"What do you propose, Sir?" the team leader asked.

"Firstly, we need to refresh the surveillance at all the main points of entry into the UK as best we can. Re-circulate the latest picture and details we have of Underwood to all the immigration services, ports, airports, Eurostar, that sort of thing. I know it is a bit like looking for a needle in a haystack, but you never know, we could get lucky. However, our number one objective and main priority is to find Radcliffe's mystery IT man before Underwood does, because I believe that is where Underwood will be concentrating his attention, now he has eliminated his former partner," Washbourne began.

"Any suggestions, Sir?" Greenwood asked. "We have so little to go on. Our only line of enquiry, which centred on the possibility that he had served with Radcliffe in the Intelligence Corps, pretty much hit a brick wall when we tried to look into Radcliffe's Army service history. To say the Corps was unhelpful, would be putting it mildly. Apart from advising us of a couple of his 'tour' destinations, they would only say that his work was classified, and they would not even tell us which Army units he was posted to."

"Okay, leave that with me. I will see if I can get some help with that from our 'higher ups'," Chief Superintendent Washbourne suggested. "What you can do, is up your surveillance on the accountant Williams, and monitor any visitors, phone calls or letters he receives at Strangeways. Same for his wife Abigail. As far as we are aware, Underwood has not contacted her, at least directly, which seems odd," Washbourne added.

"The latest we have on Abigail, is that she is living in a very nice three-bedroom flat, under her maiden name Russell, in Alderley Edge, having sold their house in Wilmslow for a very healthy £930,000. There have been no suspicious deposits or withdrawals from her bank accounts, at least the ones we know about, and we have been monitoring her known mobiles, social media, and email accounts, again with nothing remotely suspicious," Greenwood stated.

"Right," Washbourne continued, "so let's also expand our surveillance to all Underwood's organisation's known associates, especially the accountant who handled Radcliffe's affairs, and those two brothers who ran the transport company in Liverpool - McConnell's wasn't it?"

"Yes Sir," DI Greenwood confirmed.

"They went back a long way together, and I would be surprised if they were not still in touch somehow; in fact, Underwood may have used them to facilitate Radcliffe's death. Let me know if you require any more resources Richard, manpower or budgetary, and let's see if we can't finally lay our hands on Jonathon T Underwood before he causes us any more grief; third time lucky so to speak. So if you have nothing further to add gentlemen, I will let you get on with your investigations," Chief Superintendent Washourne concluded and brought the meeting to an end. The five detectives rose as one and left the conference room together, leaving the Chief Superintendent alone with his thoughts.

Chapter 2

One month after receiving the text informing him of the 'execution' of the two contracts, Jonathon T Underwood, aka Jones, was again sat at his office desk with the phone for his 'private' business in his hand, about to text Andre Botha his next assignment.

It was Andre who, with his contacts within the Dubai Royal Family, had helped the English solicitor set up a legitimate legal practice in Dubai, using his university law degree and legal experience back in the UK, simply by changing all the relevant paperwork back to his real family name of Jones (the name he now went by in Dubai) instead of Underwood, the name he had assumed by deed poll at university. Thus creating JTJ Solicitors of Dubai, sole legal practitioner and consultant to one of the minor Royals, a distant cousin of the Crown Prince, for all matters relating to English law and any legal problems arising from his Sheik's annual trips to England for the summer Flat Racing season, along with a large portion of the rest of the Dubai Royal Family. It was an appointment which necessitated Jonathon travelling to London anonymously with his employer every year as part of his diplomatic entourage. So far, Jonathon had made two successful trips to London in that capacity without raising any alarms with the forces of law and order, who were still, to the best of his knowledge, scouring the world for him and, hopefully for them, his subsequent capture and prosecution for a number of alleged criminal offences. Unlike his former friend and business partner Emrys Williams, Jonathon had not resorted to plastic surgery to alter his appearance to further hinder his potential captors' search; he had simply cut his hair to what is commonly called a crewcut, or 'number 2' all over, grown a full, dark brown beard (definitely not out of place amongst his new surroundings and employers) and taken to wearing thick, silver-framed designer glasses with clear glass.

He retrieved Andre's number from his contact list, selected 'message' and typed "Please could you call me on this number at your earliest convenience to discuss a new assignment. JTJ" before pressing the 'send' icon.

Forty-five minutes later, the same phone played the first few bars of 'Wishing Well' by Free, announcing an incoming call from an 'International Caller'. Jonathon accepted the call and waited for the caller to announce themself, which Andre Botha duly did.

"Good afternoon Andre, I trust you are well?" Jonathon then asked.

"I am, thank you Jonathon. What can I do for you?" the CEO of Security Contractors (London) Limited replied.

"Andre, I am coming over to the UK next Spring again for the Flat Season with the Royal Family, and I would be grateful if you could locate the whereabouts of a few people who I would like to visit while I am over there. The first two should be straightforward, but the third will be a lot more difficult, even for you."

"Who are they?" Andre enquired.

"The first two are my wife Abigail, who I believe is now living in an apartment in Alderley Edge under her maiden name of Russell, after selling our house in Wilmslow, and the second person is Malcolm Woolhouse, who was the head of Woolhouse & Co., which was based in Winsford, Cheshire and was our now-deceased Chief Superintendent's accountant," Underwood replied. "I believe he closed his business shortly after Jonny Radcliffe's trial and moved out of the area. I know it is a bit of a long shot, but I would like to have a chat with him regarding Jonny's financial dealings; the ones he did not divulge to the police during the investigation. In both cases, please do not contact them, as I just want to confirm their present addresses and any contact details you can find."

"That does sound quite straightforward," Andre agreed. "And the other person?"

"The other person will be far more difficult I fear," answered the solicitor. "The police looked long and hard for him, unsuccessfully I believe, and he could be anywhere in the world. He is the person I most want to find as he is in possession of a large amount of my money, over nine million pounds plus the interest it will have accrued since my timely disappearance. He will also be especially nervous of his identity and address being discovered following Radcliffe's death in prison. He will assume, correctly, that it was not suicide and that he might well be on a similar list for retribution. In his case, if you are successful in finding him, I need you to contact him on my behalf and reassure him that his whereabouts will remain hidden, and his life is under no threat from me.

He can keep the money that he managed and 'inherited' on the policeman's death, from Radcliffe's personal offshore holdings, which they made prior to our partnership. I just want the money that he and the ex-Chief Superintendent took from me and my associates. If he agrees, I will contact him directly, however or wherever he suggests. He will no doubt seek some assurances regarding his safety if he complies, which of course you will give him. But you must also assure him, if necessary, that non-compliance will certainly lead to dire consequences for him."

"Intriguing Jonathon, and who is this mystery man?" the South African asked.

"He is, or should say was, Radcliffe's IT and electronic surveillance and security expert, and he was the guy who handled all the international money laundering and wire transfers for the police officer, and then our little partnership after we joined forces, so to speak. We know that he went under the fictitious name of Martin O'Connor, and probably lived in London at the time of the initial arrests. We are pretty sure that he had been with Radcliffe for a long time, and probably served with him in the Intelligence Corps in a senior IT capacity. He probably left the Army around the same time as Radcliffe and helped set up his criminal intelligence network with him. Emrys, my ex-partner-in-crime has given me a detailed physical description from O'Connor's visit to the house in Chester, when he set up Emrys's security network there. I will email you that after our call," concluded the solicitor.

"Not much to go on Jonathon, but I will see what I can do," Andre said after a brief pause. "I will be back in touch as soon as I have anything. Regarding payment, as this is not my normal assignment, how do you suggest I bill you?"

"Howsoever you think most appropriate, Andre. I am quite happy to leave that in your hands. Invoice me whenever you require additional funds. I will deposit five thousand pounds in the usual account immediately as a downpayment," answered Jonathon and after Andre accepted the solicitor's financial arrangement, the two men said their goodbyes and ended the call.

Chapter 3

Andre Botha arranged a meeting on the afternoon following his call from the exiled solicitor Underwood, with the head of the private investigation firm he often used when he needed information regarding a potential target. Like Andre's security firm, Pimlico Investigations Limited, which was sited on the third floor of a modern six floor office block just North of the Thames, half a mile from Vauxhall Bridge, had two sides to its business. Primarily, it was a thriving, officially licensed private investigations company, but it also provided a second 'off-the-books service' to people like Andre or anyone else, once vetted, who wanted someone or something found unofficially, and was prepared to pay a little extra for it.

The two men arranged to meet at 2:30pm that afternoon, in a pub they both knew across the river in Vauxhall. Andre arrived fifteen minutes early, and was already sitting with a glass of fresh orange in one of the small four-seater alcoves at the rear of the lounge bar when Stafford Ecob, the head and founder of Pimlico Investigations, entered The Rose and Crown at precisely 2:30pm. Stafford went to the bar and ordered a half pint of Estrella, before joining Andre in the alcove. The pub was quite busy, and the two similar four-seater alcoves on either side of them were fully occupied with what looked like office workers, noisily enjoying an extended liquid lunch, completely oblivious of the two suited businessmen sat in the alcove between them.

"Good afternoon Stafford and thank you for coming on such short notice," the South African greeted the new arrival without getting up.

"No problem Andre, always happy to see you. What have you got for me this time?" the ex-army Captain and managing director of Pimlico Investigations asked, after he had sat down across the table from the South African.

"A couple of jobs; well three to be exact. The first two are straightforward, just present addresses and contact details for a couple of civilians who should be easy to trace, but the third person is something a little out of the ordinary Stafford. However, I am sure well within your compass," Andre replied. "There is no rush for the details of the first two, so you don't need to get back to me until you have something on the third target."

"I'm intrigued Andre, do continue," Stafford said leaning forward towards his South African friend and business associate, as the noise level from the two adjoining alcoves increased another notch.

"All the details are in here," Andre began, taking out a sealed, white business DL envelope and passing it to the private investigator, who immediately folded it in half and put it into the inside pocket of his dark Crombie overcoat, which he had taken off before sitting down and placed beside himself on the semi-circular bench seat. "The third person in question, however, will definitely be trying to stay as anonymous and out-of-sight as possible. He may be living anywhere in the UK or possibly abroad, we don't know. He may be living under his own or an assumed name, again we don't know."

"Not much to go on," Stafford said with a smile.

"I know," Andre agreed, "but what we do think is that this person served with Jonny Radcliffe in the Army Intelligence Corps for some time, and left the Corps around the same time as the then Major Radcliffe, who subsequently joined the Met before transferring up to the Cheshire Constabulary. As I am sure you know from the recent newspaper headlines and stories, Radcliffe was charged and found guilty of various criminal charges and sent to Strangeways, where he was found hanging in his cell. The man we are looking for, we believe, was an IT specialist in the Corps and a good friend of Radcliffe. What we would like you to do is find out as much as you can about Radcliffe's service in the Corps, where he served, which units he was attached to and any close friends, especially IT specialists, and anyone that left the service around the same time as Radcliffe. Hopefully that will lead you to the man we need to find. You will also need to tread very carefully in your investigation, because we don't know if this person still has any friends or contacts in the Corps, and we don't want to spook him and send him further underground; under no circumstances can you make any contact with this man. Please just find out who this man is, and any background information regarding his potential whereabouts."

"Understood Andre. I still have a few people I know at Army Personnel Records, and I'll ask around a few of our ex-army lads to see if they have any Intelligence Corps contacts. I'll get back to you when I have anything concrete on him. The first two should only be a couple of days, but the third will definitely take somewhat longer."

"Fine, I presume normal terms? Two thousand up front for initial expenses to the usual account and then invoices as applicable?" asked the South African.

"Perfect Andre, always good to do business with you," the private investigator replied and with that the two men finished their drinks, stood up, shook hands and then left the pub together.

Chapter 4

The day following Jonathon's discussions with Andre Botha, his 'special contracts' business contact, he was just about to leave his office when one of his private PAYG phones, which he kept in the top right-hand drawer of his desk, 'pinged' to announce an incoming message. He put down the briefcase he had just picked up and opened the drawer to see which phone it was. He saw that it was the black iPhone 12S, which he knew was the one he used to contact his friend and ex-business associate Declan McConnell, the MD of McConnell's Transport & Warehousing based in Liverpool. He knew it must be important for Declan to contact him directly, so he immediately picked up the phone and opened the message, which simply said, "Please contact at first opportunity on the usual number."

The solicitor retrieved the only number in the phone's directory, another PAYG phone, and pressed the 'call' icon. Declan answered the call on the first ring.

"Thanks for calling back so promptly Jonathon," Declan answered immediately.

"I presumed it was important Declan, what's up?" asked the concerned solicitor.

"I have just had a very worrying text myself on my private phone, the one I use for non-official business. It said that the sender hoped Jimmy and myself were both well, and Fergus sends his best regards. It then read "We have long memories" and finally a picture of an Irish Tricolour. I think the timing is too much of a co-incidence not to be connected to the recent death of Radcliffe, the smuggled gemstones and our removal of those three over at Larne in Northern Ireland. Radcliffe's death must have jogged a few unpleasant memories in someone over there, and to add to that, I have been trying to get in touch with Fergus over in Belfast, but he is not answering his phone. I spoke to his brother, and he hasn't seen him for a couple of days, which is both unusual and also a cause for concern," Declan informed the solicitor, who was a major silent shareholder in his and his twin brother's transport and warehousing business.

"That is indeed worrying Declan, the last thing we need is interference from across the Irish Sea, especially prior to my impending visit to the UK next Spring. You will obviously keep trying to contact your cousin and let me know any developments. Please be extra careful; if Fergus has been persuaded to divulge our connection to those three deaths, it could prove very dangerous for all of us, especially you and your brother."

"I agree Jonathon. As soon as I hear anything from Belfast, I will let you know," Declan confirmed.

With that the two men promised to keep in touch and ended the call.

Chapter 5

It was Detective Inspector Richard Greenwood who called the second team meeting with his boss, Chief Superintendent Geoff Washbourne. They met in the same conference room in New Scotland Yard at 9:30am on a rainy Monday morning.

Once the five investigating officers had helped themselves to the tea or coffee provided on a side table, and sat down again at the same large oval conference table, CS Washbourne, who had already been seated at the table when the five officers had entered the room together, greeted them all and began the meeting.

"I presume you have something for me Richard?" the Chief Superintendent asked expectantly.

"Yes Sir, it is a bit of a curiosity; it may be something, it may not be. As you know, we have widened our electronic surveillance to cover the McConnell brothers over in Liverpool, and DC Bell came across a text sent recently to Declan McConnell on one of the two iPhones he uses, his personal one for non-business traffic. It was from a withheld number, probably a PAYG phone, and it said that the sender hoped that his brother Jimmy and himself were both well, and Fergus, his cousin over in Belfast, sent his best regards. It then read "We have long memories," and finally a picture of an Irish Tricolour. It might be a coincidence, but we think coming so soon after Jonny Radcliffe's death, it might be that old wounds have been re-opened with certain people across the water in Belfast. We are pretty sure that those three Irish bodies, over at the farmhouse in Larne, are connected to Underwood's gemstone smuggling operation, and that the solicitor probably had them killed in retribution for them relieving him, with help from that driver at Wade's Manufacturing, of the precious stones from their last delivery. If so, and if some people in Belfast have discovered that the McConnell brothers and Underwood were involved, then that could be a serious problem for the three of them. As we know, the criminal fraternity in Belfast would not take kindly to having some of their own executed by people from our side of the Irish Sea. Having said that, we don't know if the Irish side have definite proof of Underwood and his people's involvement, or if they are just on a 'fishing expedition', so to speak."

"Interesting Richard, as you said. Keep an eye on that and see if there are any developments. I still think that it is a strong possibility that Underwood has had, and is still, getting help from the McConnells in some way. I presume you haven't picked up any other potential traffic between the brothers and Underwood, following the text or through general traffic?" Washbourne asked.

"No Sir, not through any of the phones or email addresses which we are aware of," answered DI Greenwood.

"Okay if that's all, I'll let you get on with your work," and Washbourne wound up the meeting.

Chapter 6

Andre Botha received his first contact from the head of Pimlico Investigations three weeks after their meeting at The Rose and Crown in Vauxhall. It was a text message on his private iPhone, the one he used for 'off-the-books' business and it simply said, "Biking first report over to you this PM. SE".

The sealed A4 brown jiffy bag duly arrived at his office reception at 4:30pm in the hands of a helmeted dispatch rider. The receptionist signed for the delivery and took it straight through to the office of the head of the security company. She knocked on his door before entering carrying the jiffy bag.

"The delivery you were expecting Mr Botha," the receptionist said and handed the package to the seated Managing Director.

"Thank you Kim. By the way, did your husband get that new job he was applying for?" asked the South African.

"Yes he did, thank you Sir. Wayne starts it in about six weeks after serving his notice with the council."

"Excellent Kim, give him my congratulations and I hope it goes well for him," Andre said and the receptionist returned to her position behind the counter at the reception, closing the door on her way out.

Once she had left his office, Andre opened the jiffy bag and took out the typed report. As expected, Pimlico

Investigations had had no problem finding all the contact details for Underwood's wife and the now retired head of the defunct Woolhouse and Co. accountants, and they were all there on the first page of the report. The findings for the second part of the three page report, as anticipated, were less complete. The two pages did, however, contain a complete history of Major Jonny Radcliffe's service record in the Intelligence Corps from the day of entry until he left just over fifteen years later. It listed where he served each tour, the dates he was there and which units he served in. There followed a short note to say that Stafford Ecob's investigation company was now trying to find any close friend and IT specialist who served alongside Radcliffe, and had handed his papers in around the same time as the ex-Major. This, Stafford acknowledged, would probably take a lot longer and he assured Andre that he would be in touch as soon as he had some concrete news.

Andre sat back in his chair and considered whether to forward the report to Jonathon Underwood, his employer for this contract. After several minutes he decided to wait for more information regarding the elusive IT man, before returning the report to the jiffy bag and placing it in the bottom drawer, marked T – Z, of a light grey metallic filing cabinet, which was solely used for his 'off-the-books' contract work.

It was five weeks later that Andre finally received the much anticipated second report, again in a sealed brown A4 Jiffy bag and delivered to his office by despatch rider, but it was worth the wait.

He took out the detailed report, and read it slowly with mounting satisfaction. It was obvious that the target had not been easy to identify, and Pimlico had not actually located his present whereabouts as yet, but they were pretty confident they had discovered who he was, from the information and physical description given to them by the South African, and three different properties which were owned by him. The first, which they believed was his main residence, was a large, three-bedroomed flat in Knightsbridge, which was owned, as the other two properties were, under the name of Brian Connelly. The second property was a small semi-detached house in Newcastle-upon-Tyne, the place where he was born and only half a mile from St. James' Park, the home of his beloved Newcastle United, and the third and final property they had so far discovered was a two-bedroomed detached holiday home in Little Coxwell, a small village just outside Faringdon in the Cotswolds.

Connelly, the report disclosed, had joined the Army from school after completing his 'A' levels, done his basic army training at Catterick before joining the Intelligence Corps and being sent down to Templar Barracks in Ashford, Kent. He had joined four years earlier than Radcliffe, who had come straight from Sandhurst to the Corps, and they had met during Radcliffe's first tour to Northern Ireland, Pimlico had discovered. They then subsequently served together in units in Cyprus, Minden in Germany, attached to BRIXMIS in West Berlin a couple of years before the Wall came down, and on a couple more tours in Northern Ireland during the latter part of 'The Troubles'. Having found out where they had been stationed, and speaking to some of the soldiers who had served with Radcliffe and

Connelly, they had confirmed they were good friends, kept themselves to themselves and that Connelly was well known for his IT expertise, even amongst the Intelligence Corps specialists. Connelly, who by then was a Staff Sergeant, had put his papers in six months before Radcliffe left the Army to join the Metropolitan Police's Counter Terrorism Unit. There was then a gap of ten years before Connelly reappeared, when he bought the apartment in Knightsbridge and started doing voluntary work with the London-based Veterans Community Group. He had donated a large amount of computer equipment including screens, terminals and printers and set up the systems for their administration staff, as well as spending many hours training them and holding beginners' courses for interested veterans at the Group's offices. A couple of Pimlico's operatives were ex-servicemen, which combined with Stafford's contact in the Army personnel department, is how they had been able to gather so much information regarding Radcliffe and Connelly's service history. The two ex-servicemen had also visited the Vet's offices under the guise of looking for help and engaging with some of the other vets there, who were happy to sing the praises of Connelly, after the undercover operatives said they had known him when their paths had crossed on some of their own tours. The investigators also discovered that Connelly regularly went back home to Newcastle, to watch his beloved football team when they were not playing in London, but that he had not been seen at the Vet's offices for a couple of months; in fact coincidently, from about the same time that Jonny Radcliffe had been found hanging in his cell in Strangeways.

The report concluded by saying that Pimlico would now embark on trying to actually determine Connelly's present location, and report back as soon as anything definite had been discovered.

Andre re-read the report before texting a brief message to Jonathon Underwood. The text read "Excellent news. Contact details of first two targets found and confident identity of third target discovered. Will email copy of full details and report ASAP."

Chapter 7

Andre received the third and final report from Pimlico Investigations just over three weeks after the second report. It was brief and concluded that, after having had surveillance teams at the three properties they had identified as belonging to the target Brian Connelly, either he had further residences they had not discovered, or more likely that he had gone to ground following Radcliffe's death. They had watched the residences twenty-four hours a day for the three weeks, and the target had not been seen; also, there had been no activity whatsoever, either in or out of the homes.

After filing the report along with the previous two, Andre took out a PAYG phone, one of a batch of ten he had recently purchased, and texted an update to the exiled Manchester solicitor in Dubai. It read, "No activity at target's homes. If OK with you will access them and try to contact him with invitation to talk."

Ten minutes later that same phone 'pinged' with an incoming message, which simply had the 'thumbs-up' emoji as a reply.

Andre immediately summoned his Operations Director to his office, and instructed him to organise three infiltration teams of two people each to enter the London, Newcastle and Little Coxwell properties. They were to carry out a thorough search of the said properties, photographing anything that might give them an idea of the owner's current whereabouts. They were not to be concerned about hiding the fact that the properties had been searched, as he wanted the owner to know that they had been. They were also to assume that the properties would probably have sophisticated alarm and surveillance systems installed, but again that should not be a concern to the teams, as the owner would certainly not want any involvement from the police. The three teams were to co-ordinate their searches to enter the premises at the same time and provide live feeds back to the office, via body cameras, where Andre and the Operations Director would be monitoring the searches.

....

The three teams entered the homes simultaneously at 3am on the Tuesday morning of the following week, after they had all carried out a preliminary examination of the exterior of the properties during the Monday afternoon, looking for any signs of security systems and having found none. What they did not know initially, was that as soon as each team had entered their respective property, they had sent a silent alarm to a laptop which was sitting open and active on a table in a house in Scotland, having stood on one of the many pressure pads, distributed throughout the three homes under rugs and mats in each room. They were also captured on the very small keyhole video cameras, which were hidden throughout the three premises, as the unwanted visitors moved from room to room, searching as they went.

Brian Connelly was awoken immediately the first alarm sounded on his laptop, put on his dressing gown and flip-flops before going through to the kitchen of the three-bedroom bungalow he had taken on a long-term let just outside Dumfries, shortly after Jonny Radcliffe's suspicious death in Strangeways Prison. He watched in silence, as the three teams went from room to room in his three homes. There was no sound relay on his systems, but he could see that one member of each team seemed to be talking into a microphone headset throughout their search, and that he was wearing a body camera attached to the front of his black bomber jacket. Each of the intruders was also wearing a black ski-mask and black gloves, making possible future identification of them extremely difficult.

As Connelly was watching in his kitchen, Andre Botha and his Operations Director were watching the bodycam footage, and listening to the commentary from his three team leaders, in his office in central London. The teams soon discovered the pressure pads and the various video cameras capturing their every move and reported this back to Andre, confirming he probably was not the only interested party watching the night's operations; in fact, it was exactly what Andre had hoped for. When the teams had concluded their searches, having found nothing which might indicate Connelly's present whereabouts, Andre instructed each of his team leaders to hold up the message he had previously instructed them to write on a large piece of white paper and take with them, to one of the security cameras in each of the three properties. The message said "A mutual colleague would like to talk. Please call me on this number," which was followed by the number of one of the South African's new, unused PAYG phones. The three teams then all left their respective premises, making sure they were locked and secure before they went.

The PAYG phone on Andre's desk rang five minutes later, and smiling, the South African picked it up and answered. "Good morning Brian, thank you for calling so promptly."

"No problem," Connelly replied, "I have been expecting your contact," and then he went silent, waiting for the inevitable instructions from who, he presumed, was the boss of his early morning visitors.

"First of all, our mutual colleague would like to assure you that if you agree to his request, then you are in no danger whatsoever, not from him anyway," Andre began. "He would like to open a dialogue with you, either face to face or by phone or email, whichever you are most comfortable with, in order to facilitate the return of the property of his which you are currently holding."

"What property would that be?" Connelly asked, knowing the answer, but continuing before Andre could answer, "and what reassurances would he give if I comply, as it appears that you are very efficient at finding the identity and location of someone who would rather remain hidden and anonymous."

"He simply wants the return of the monies that you and your ex-partner stole from him, plus the accrued interest of course. You keep everything you made with him before you formed your new partnership with my client which, he presumes, you have now 'inherited' on his death. As to assurances, he can only collect his monies if you are alive, and he is sure you will now take certain steps to publish what you know regarding my client, should anything happen to you after the transfer. So, it would be in both your interests to maintain the 'status quo' so to speak".

After a short silence, Connelly finally replied to the South African, "It would seem that I have little choice other than to agree, as I presume that if I don't, then I would more than likely suffer the same fate as my former partner. I will get back to you shortly, and we can make the necessary arrangements," he agreed, and then ended the call, hoping to buy himself some time to consider his options. He had been shocked at how quickly Underwood, or at least whoever he had employed, had discovered his identity and location.

Andre immediately took out another PAYG phone and texted Jonathon Underwood in Dubai, "Have made contact with the target who is willing to talk. Await your further instructions."

Underwood returned his colleague's call the following afternoon.

"Great work, Andre," the solicitor said after the two businessmen had exchanged greetings. "What happened?" he asked, being forewarned of the impending operation the previous night.

"The three residences were empty as anticipated, but were all monitored via CCTV and alarm pressure pads, which were connected via Wi-Fi and the internet, I presume, to a remote monitoring system, or more likely

Connelly's laptop. I had instructed the three team leaders to take a written message and contact number, in case of such an eventuality, in order to hold it up to one of the cameras. Connelly duly obliged within ten minutes by calling the cell phone."

"Excellent Andre, well done," Underwood congratulated him.

"How would you like me to proceed Jonathon?" the South African asked.

"If possible, I would still like you to find our elusive IT man. That would certainly help if he foolishly decides to try and be less than helpful. Other than that, wait for his call as there is no rush on my side - in fact, the longer he tries to drag out a conclusion to our business, the better it suits me at the moment," suggested the solicitor.

"Alright Jonathon, while we wait for his call I will continue to keep a round-the-clock surveillance on the three properties. Now that he knows that we know where they are, and that we are looking to arrange a meeting, he might return to one of them thinking we are probably not interested in them anymore. It is a bit of a long shot, but if he does, we can follow him, see what he is up to, and perhaps find out where he is living now," Andre suggested.

"Again, excellent idea Andre. Will speak soon," and they ended the call.

Chapter 8

Andre instructed his three two-man surveillance teams in Newcastle, London and the Cotswolds to continue their 24 hour watch on the three residences, at least for the immediate future, promising to spell them with three new teams in a couple of weeks.

Fortuitously, the proposed change of watchers was not required, as the following Saturday, around midday, the two operatives in Newcastle, both of whom were Geordies and ex-military themselves, watched Brian Connelly calmly walk up to the door of his semi-detached house, insert his key into the front door Yale lock and walk inside, pulling a medium sized black case on rollers by an extended handle and carrying a black knapsack over his right shoulder, the type used for a laptop and its accompanying accessories. The two operatives were in a silver Ford Focus parked about fifty metres down the road in a long-stay Euro carpark.

One of the two watchers immediately sent a text to the Operations Director, informing him of the target's arrival at his Newcastle home and requesting instructions on what they should do.

Five minutes later, he received a message informing the two men to hold a watching brief, follow the target wherever he went and report back anything of interest immediately. They acknowledged their instructions and then had a brief discussion on how they should proceed.

As Connelly had arrived on foot, they decided to split up; one of them would remain in the car and the second watcher get a window table in the all-day café at the other end of the street, which meant they could follow him on foot or by car, depending on whether he walked out or called a taxi.

They did not have long to wait, as just an hour after going into his house Connelly re-emerged, wearing a black and white scarf and matching knitted bob hat, both with Newcastle United emblazoned on them. Connelly then walked towards St James' Park, disappearing into a large black and white timber-framed pub called 'The Geordie Lads', which was full of other Newcastle United supporters, who were spilling out onto the adjoining footpath and road, just a hundred metres from the ground. Being from that city and having their native accent, the two followers separately followed Connelly into the pub and saw him meet up with what were obviously a group of his mates and fellow supporters. After a couple of quick pints, Connelly left the pub in the company of five others and sang their way down to one of the home team supporters' entrances, and then into the ground. The two watchers noted the entrance number, and casually returned to their car to report back to the Operations Director.

As soon as Andre Botha was told of their main target's sighting, he immediately ordered the two watchers at the London residence to gather their overnight bags and drive up to Newcastle, to join the team already there. They were to assist in following the target and increase their surveillance capability, whilst lessening the chance of Connelly spotting that he was being followed.

The two watchers in-situ at St. James' Park were back outside the entrance Connelly had used, well before the game finished and were on hand as he re-appeared, jubilantly singing with his five friends as he exited the ground, triumphant after his team had easily beaten Everton 3 – 0.

The two watchers followed their target back to 'The Geordie Lads', where he spent the next couple of hours before walking, rather unsteadily, back to his house. The watchers saw the curtains drawn and lights turned on in the downstairs rooms, and twenty minutes later a delivery man on a motorbike stopped outside the house, rang the bell and handed in a large flat box and a couple of cartons to Connelly, before driving off again as the front door was closed, and Connelly went back inside to enjoy his evening meal. Two hours later, the watchers saw the upstairs lights come on and the downstairs ones turned off, signalling that their target was almost certainly going to bed, and decided that nothing was going to be happening until the following day.

The watchers had been informed of the imminent arrival of their two colleagues, so one of the pair walked back to their room at the hotel where they were staying to await their arrival, while the second one remained in the car watching Connelly's house, which was now in complete darkness.

The two additional watchers arrived at the hotel in the early hours of Sunday morning, and immediately agreed to get their heads down for about the next six hours after their long drive up from London, while the other original Newcastle operative returned to his colleague watching the house. The two new arrivals would then take over the surveillance in the Ford Focus at 8.00am, allowing the two original watchers to return to the hotel for some sleep themselves.

As arranged, the new arrivals took over the surveillance the next morning, after a quiet night without any further movement from Connelly inside the house. The two Geordie colleagues then returned to their hotel, placed the 'Do Not Disturb' sign on the outside handles of their room doors and immediately went to bed for some well-earned sleep.

Having had no contact from their new colleagues watching the house, the two Geordies met in the foyer of the hotel four hours later, and then walked to the café at the other end of the street from their colleagues in the Euro carpark. They ordered a late full English breakfast with plenty of toast and a large pot of tea, which they ate slowly, whilst also keeping an eye on the house along with their associates down the road.

Just as they were finishing the last of the toast and a second cup of tea each, the front door of Connelly's house opened and he re-appeared, pulling his suitcase and carrying his laptop backpack. He checked he had locked the front door before turning right, towards the two watchers in the café. As soon as he did, the mobile phone laid on the table between the two men rang and on answering it, the voice of one of the new arrivals, now sat in the car, announced, "Target leaving the house and heading your way on foot."

"Yes, we see him," replied one of the two men sat at the café table. "You two follow and we will come after you. Normal four-man box procedure and be very careful, this man is an ex- Intelligence Officer, and let's see where he's going."

"Roger that" came the reply, and the four-man surveillance team moved smoothly into position, two on each side of the road as Connelly walked briskly towards the city centre.

Five minutes later, one of the native Geordies and the team leader, who was behind Connelly on the opposite side of the road, spoke into the concealed microphone which was attached to the small two-way radio in his inside pocket, "I think he's going to the train station. I'm going to get ahead and be there when he arrives. I can cut through the shopping arcade and then leg it round to the station and be there before him. I'll stand by the ticket office and machines in case he has to buy a ticket. If he goes straight onto a platform, we'll follow him onto whichever train he catches and get a ticket on the train."

"Roger that," came back from the other three two-way radios, whose owners calmly continued to follow their target, as the team leader turned right into a shopping arcade, before running down the passageway and then coming out into a large square, before sprinting down towards the main railway station, ignoring the suspicious stares from the many shoppers he passed on the way.

As anticipated, he arrived at the main entrance to the station a couple of minutes before Connelly, with his three-man surveillance team in tow, and was able to position himself next to one of the ticket machines, as if he was considering buying one. When Connelly did arrive, he walked straight passed him, through the concourse and onto one of the main platforms. The display monitor above the platform entrance showed that the train standing at the platform, which was due to leave in ten minutes time, was for Edinburgh and the destination of the train following that in twenty minutes time was for all stations to Carlisle. Connelly walked halfway down the platform and sat on one of the many benches situated along its length. He was obviously not going to Edinburgh.

Again, the team leader spoke into his microphone, "Appears not going to Edinburgh, looks like Carlisle or one of the stations on the way there. I'll go and get four singles, keep an eye on him and if he does get on that train, we follow and I'll pass out the tickets once we are all seated."

Again three "Roger that" replies sounded in his ear piece as the leader walked back to the ticket machine, to purchase their four one-way tickets to the last major English town before the Scottish border.

Chapter 9

The four-man surveillance team were scattered along the platform as the train for Carlisle pulled into the station. The team leader, known to his colleagues as Geordie for obvious reasons, spoke as the train pulled slowly to a stop. "I'll get into the same carriage as the target, the rest of you enter different ones and don't sit together, in case he has a wander down the train. I'll get out at the same station as him, and you all stay on the train and get off at the next stop and await my instructions, unless of course he goes all the way to Carlisle. If he does, again I'll initially follow him and contact you all once I get an idea as to his potential movements."

"What if he's catching another train from Carlisle?" one of the other team members asked.

"Good point Jim," Geordie answered. "In that case you and Dave get on board with him and we'll get the next train to the same destination. You two follow him if you can, as discretely as possible, and keep us informed. We'll then get to you as soon as possible."

As they finished their call, they watched Connelly get into the middle carriage of the three-carriage train and followed him on board; the team leader into the same one as their target, sitting four rows behind him on the same side of the train, two prospective followers in the front carriage and the fourth member of the team in the last carriage.

LOOSE ENDS

The train stopped several times on its journey, but Connelly remained seated throughout, finally standing and exiting his carriage at the train's destination of Carlisle. He then walked over to the large screen in the middle of the platform, which displayed the times and destinations, and relevant platform numbers, for all the imminent arrivals and departures to and from Carlisle. Having studied the display for less than a minute, he checked his watch and then, pulling his suitcase, walked over to an adjacent bench and sat down, putting his computer backpack on the floor beside him. As arranged, Jim and Dave walked separately to either end of the platform before sitting down themselves on an empty bench, whilst the team leader, who had shared Connelly's carriage, and the fourth member of the team left the station and walked a couple of hundred metres towards the town, before entering a small café to await further news from their colleagues.

Back on the platform, two trains pulled into the station five minutes apart, but Connelly remained seated. Then twenty minutes after arriving at Carlisle, Connelly finally stood up as a third train, with the destination of Dumfries in the display panel above the driver, stopped at their platform. Connelly collected his belongings, followed by his two 'shadows', and boarded the train, with Jim in the same carriage and Dave in the next one along.

Dave took out his mobile and texted to Geordie, "Target just boarded train to Dumfries."

He immediately received a reply, which was simply a 'thumbs up' emoji and then settled down to see where

Connelly's destination would turn out to be. The train stopped a couple of times, before, about thirty minutes later, pulling into Dumfries station with Connelly still on board. The three men, Connelly and his two 'tails', headed towards the exit, each showing the ticket collector the ticket they had each bought on the train during the journey. Fortunately, the train guard had approached Connelly first, and Jim, sitting a few rows behind him had overheard him asking for a single ticket to Dumfries and was able to buy a similar ticket, and also inform his fellow watcher on the train to do the same, as well as notifying his team leader back in Carlisle. This enabled their two colleagues in Carlisle to get a taxi to take them over to Dumfries, hopefully arriving not too long after the train.

As it turned out, the two in the taxi arrived at Dumfries five minutes before their colleagues, as the train had been delayed at some faulty signals for fifteen minutes and then, because of that delay, had been held up at the next station for a further ten minutes awaiting a long goods train to pass through.

When Connelly did finally arrive and step down off the train, followed by his two 'shadows', the other two members of the surveillance team were already positioned outside the station, one stood by the bus stop and one near the taxi rank. As arranged, Jim and Dave walked straight out of the station and continued off in different directions towards the town centre. Connelly exited closely behind them with his luggage and went to the taxi rank. As he gave his destination to the driver, the watcher stood close to the rank walked past him, overhearing the address destination before carrying on walking towards his colleague at the bus stop. As Connelly drove off in his taxi, Geordie was already arranging to meet up with his fellow team members at the nearby Station Hotel, before sending a text to his Operations Director which read "Have possible address for target. Will report once confirmed."

He received an immediate reply, "Excellent work. Proceed with extreme caution."

After having a late lunch at the Station Hotel, the four-man team booked two twin rooms for three nights each, before going out separately to have a walk around Dumfries, none of the four men ever having been to this particular town before. They met back at the hotel at seven o'clock where they had an evening meal, the room sharers sitting together at separate tables. They then went into the hotel bar, again separately in their pairs, before each going to their respective rooms fifteen minutes apart.

The following Monday morning at just after 10am, one member of each pair entered the premises of two separate local car hire companies and hired a car for three days: one a silver Kia Sportage and the other a grey Vauxhall Astra Estate. They then drove back to the hotel, picked up their roommate and, after checking their destination on 'Google Earth', drove out to the address which one of their team had overheard Connelly give to the taxi driver the day before. Geordie in the Kia arrived at the address first, and drove another 50 metres down the road, which consisted of a number of detached houses and bungalows, each separated by a good distance from its neighbour on either side, while the Astra stopped about the same distance before arriving at the target address. There was still an Estate Agent's sign standing in the bungalow's front garden adjacent to the road, advertising that the property was 'To Let or For Sale' and the Agent's details, including phone number and address in Dumfries. There was a black Range Rover Sport on the bungalow's driveway, with a registration plate that confirmed that it was only eighteen months old, and black tinted rear windows.

"You two go back into town to the Estate Agent and see if you can find out anything about the new tenant. Just say you were driving past the houses looking for properties for sale in the area, and had seen the sign and might be interested in buying it, okay?" the team leader instructed his colleagues in the Astra Estate. "We will hang around here, get the lay of the land and keep an eye out for the target."

"Will do. Speak soon," came the prompt reply, and the driver carefully reversed into the entrance of the drive he had stopped besides, before signalling right and returning back towards Dumfries town centre and the house's Estate Agent.

Geordie drove another 50 metres down the road, before turning around and driving back past the house and parking in the closed entrance to a large field, about 100 metres past the house, but with a good view through his rear window of the target's bungalow, using the powerful binoculars he had retrieved from his backpack in the car's boot.

Forty-five minutes later, there having been no activity at the bungalow, the team leader's two-way radio came to life, "Just visited the Estate Agent, who apologised and said that the property had been recently let on a six-month contract, and they had not had time to take the sign down," his colleague reported.

"Okay. We just need to confirm that the target is indeed living there now. We'll stay here and do the first watch. If you haven't heard from me by 2pm, bring us a couple of sandwiches and drinks and then you can spell us. If Connelly surfaces before then, we'll return to the hotel and report back to base," the team leader replied and ended the call.

At just after 12.30, Connelly emerged from the front door of the bungalow, got into the Range Rover, turned left off the drive and drove towards Dumfries, passing the two watchers in the Kia Sportage seconds later.

As soon as the Range Rover was out of sight, the two watchers in the Kia sat back up from their hunched down positions, which they had quickly adopted when they saw Connelly driving towards them. Geordie took out his mobile and texted to the Operations Director, "Target's current address confirmed in Dumfries. Returning to hotel to await further instructions."

He then sent a second text to his colleagues in Dumfries, "Target confirmed. See you back at the hotel shortly."

Chapter 10

Andre was sat at his desk in his London office when there was a knock at the door. He called "Come in," and his Operations Director opened the door and entered his boss's office, walked towards him and sat down on the chair opposite him across the desk.

"Good news I trust?" enquired the head of the security firm.

"Yes indeed, Sir," came the prompt reply. "Just had a text from our operatives following Connelly. He left his Newcastle residence yesterday and we now know that he has let a detached bungalow on the outskirts of Dumfries in the Scottish Borders. We have the address and he was seen leaving it earlier today. They have confirmed that the bungalow has been let to him on a minimum six months contract."

"Excellent. Call the team back and have them report to me once they return to the office," Andre instructed his number two.

"Will do Sir," said the Operations Director and stood up and left the office, closing the door behind him.

As soon as he had left, Andre took out one of the PAYG phones in his top right-hand desk drawer, brought up the only number in the phone's directory, accessed the 'message' icon and typed in "Target address found and confirmed. Await further instructions" and then pressed the 'send' icon.

The phone sitting on Jonathon's desk in his Dubai office 'pinged' to announce an incoming message. He finished typing the final paragraph in the legal document he was about to file on his sole client's behalf, before picking up the phone and accessing the message which had originated from an 'International Caller'. It was from Andre, and it said they had discovered and confirmed Connelly's address and awaited his further instructions.

"Brilliant Andre, well done, well done indeed," the solicitor exclaimed aloud to his empty office. "Now what to do?" he continued aloud to himself, "What should we do about our mystery IT man?"

After quite a long period of silent reflection, Jonathon made a decision and texted back to his business colleague in London. "Great work Andre, you have excelled yourself once again. When Connelly finally gets back in touch with you, let me know how he intends to proceed and I will take it from there. After that, please send me the final invoice for your excellent services, and then I will be back in touch if I require anything further. Once again, many thanks," and returned the phone to his desk drawer.

Chapter 11

The morning after his return from watching his beloved Newcastle United, and many fitful nights' sleep following his very disturbing telephone conversation with the head of the firm who had not only discovered his identity, but his three separate residences, Connelly finally gave up trying to sleep, and at 6:30am he got up, had a shower, dressed, and went through into the kitchen to make himself some breakfast. As he did every morning, after his mandatory first cup of tea of the day, he put two Weetabix into a cereal bowl, along with 50gms of low-sugar nuts and seeds granola, a handful of grapes and some semi-skimmed milk. His mind was in overdrive, as he slowly ate his nourishing first meal of the day. How had they found his identity and all the homes so quickly, who were they, presuming 'they' had been engaged by Underwood, where was Underwood, what were Underwood's ultimate plans for him and most importantly, what could he do about the situation he now found himself in? These questions whirled around and around in his mind as he ate, with no explanations or answers readily springing to mind. He finally finished his breakfast, washed the mug, bowl and spoon and left them on the draining board of the sink. He then went through to the main lounge and sat down on the large, two-seater leather sofa, which faced the large bay window that looked out over the front garden of the bungalow, picking up a small note pad and pen from the glass-topped coffee table in front of him, as he sat down.

He was an inveterate planner, and always compiled a list of his proposed actions, whenever confronted with a problem or set of situations to overcome; something he had learnt in the Intelligence Corps and carried through into his civilian life.

Once settled into his problem-solving mindset, he went through the situation he now found himself him and made notes accordingly which, as always, were split into two categories: firstly, 'unanswered questions' and secondly, 'actions to be taken'.

Questions:

1. What are Underwood's plans for me, apart from retrieving his money?
2. Do I return the money immediately or stall?
3. Once the money is returned, am I in danger as in 1 above?
4. How can I mitigate any danger in 3 above?
5. Where is Underwood?
6. Who are the people he has employed to find me?

Actions:

1. Find out who had found him.
2. Through 1 above, try to locate Underwood's whereabouts.
3. GO ON THE OFFENSIVE!

The ex-Intelligence Corps Staff Sergeant looked over his brief list of questions, and proposed actions for a few minutes, formulating an action plan as he did.

The opposition, which in his mind Underwood had become, knew about his three residences and had issued him with his demands, so he decided immediately that he no longer needed to remain in hiding in Dumfries; although he would retain the bungalow as a possible bolt hole for the time being, unaware that Underwood had already discovered that location as well. Connelly's second decision, following on from his first, was that he would return to his main residency in London, where his state-of-the-art computer network was housed, and where he could mount his own search for the opposition. From there, he would use his own network of contacts, both legal and criminal if necessary, to attempt to uncover the identity of the people who had so quickly and efficiently tracked him down and, perhaps through them, discover their employer Underwood's new place of residence, which he was pretty sure was somewhere abroad. Once in possession of this information, he would then be in a much stronger position, not necessarily in retaining the money, but more importantly as a bargaining chip to ensure his own future safety, once he eventually returned Underwood's ill-gotten gains to him. He also decided to stall returning the money for as long as possible, in order to give him as much time as possible to discover Underwood's whereabouts, without trying Underwood's patience too much.

Having formulated his initial plan, Connelly felt much better about the situation he now found himself in, and quickly packed everything he would need into his suitcase and laptop bag. He then had a quick check round the bungalow, before loading the two bags into the boot of his Range Rover, locked the front door, and then got into his car. He turned left off the drive, back towards Dumfries and his ultimate destination of London, not noticing what appeared to be an empty silver Kia Sportage, parked about a hundred metres down the road, as he drove passed it seconds later, concentrating on the road ahead, and the plans he was making for when he would finally arrive at his London apartment.

Chapter 12

Connelly arrived back at his London apartment in the early evening, after a couple of service station stops and a reasonably uneventful, albeit long and tedious, drive down from Dumfries. Thankfully, his late-night visitors had not left the place in a mess, although they had not made any effort to cover up their search, so it did not take him long to get everything back to some semblance of normality. After a quick snack from the fridge, he then had a shower, before deciding to have an early night, ready to put his plans into action the following morning.

He got up at his usual time of 7am, the alarm clock in his head all that was necessary to wake him, something he did every morning without fail, whether he had things to do or not.

After his usual initial cup of tea followed by breakfast, he then took out his notebook and set out his objectives for the day. This process helped him clarify in his mind exactly what he intended to do, and the order he would do it in. After a brief pause, he wrote:

1. Go to Vets Community Group for catch up, and be openly visible for any potential 'watchers'.
2. Locate whereabouts of ex-Captain Tony Cunningham.
3. Arrange/have meeting with TC.
4. Edit CCTV footage from intruders' searches of properties.
5. Call mobile, to confirm money transfer/perhaps offer to meet, and buy some time.

He looked over his 'to do' list, nodded to himself, and then got his coat before heading over to Lewisham, where the Veterans Group had its office and 'walk-in' centre, in the local Community Centre. The Group was run by Major (Ret'd) Peter Whyatt, ex-Coldstream Guards, and had been since its inception fifteen years earlier, six months after Whyatt finally retired from the Army, following twenty-three distinguished years' service.

When Connelly entered the Major's office, he was immediately welcomed by the Commanding Officer, "Well look what the cat's dragged in," Whyatt exclaimed, smiling on seeing Connelly. "Where the hell have you been for the last couple of months?"

"Sorry I've not been in touch Sir, but I've been abroad on a little job I got presented with," replied Connelly. "I know I should have let you know, but it was all a bit of a rush, sorry."

"No harm done. It was obviously nowhere sunny looking at your pale complexion," joked Whyatt, "where was it?"

"Nowhere interesting; anything for me while I was away?" Connelly asked, changing the subject.

"Nothing imminent. We've had a couple of enquiries about your 'IT for Beginners', but not enough interest yet for another course," Whyatt replied. "If we get some more, I'll let you know. It's a minimum of six you prefer in order to run a course, isn't it?"

"Yes, if possible," Connelly agreed. "Talking about courses, do you remember that officer I helped set up in business with his IT network, about eighteen months ago, ex-Captain Cunningham from the Fusiliers? It was a security and private investigation company he started, with a couple of other Vets from the Centre. Do you know if he's still in business and, if so, do you have his contact details? I might have a job for him."

"Hang on, I'll have a quick look. I'm pretty sure it is a going concern - in fact, I remember he came back to me about six months ago, as he had a couple of new vacancies and asked if I could recommend anyone from here," the Major replied, as he stood up and went over to one of the silver, three-drawer filing cabinets which, along with his desk and the two chairs, took up most of the floor space in the small office.

"Cunningham you said," Whyatt said half to himself, as he looked along the cabinets before opening the top drawer of the second one, and taking out one of the 'hanging' files. "Here we are, Captain Anthony Cunningham," as he read the name on the front of the buff-coloured file, before opening it on the desk in front of him. He then quietly read through the couple of pages of typed information, before looking up again at the interested ex-Army Intelligence Corps Staff Sergeant. "Yes, he was certainly still in business six months ago when, as I said, he popped in to enquire if we had anyone suitable for a couple of vacancies he had. In fact, I made a note saying he had expanded his business, and appeared to be making a go of it. There was one ex-soldier we had on our books who had served in 'The Regiment', after doing five years in the Paras, before handing his papers in. Ended up on the streets after drink and drug problems, a common enough story unfortunately, before turning up here. Don't know if Cunningham took him on, but he had cleaned himself up by then with our help. Right, let's see his contact details," Major Whyatt continued. "Yes, here we are, the firm is called 'Guards Security & Investigations Limited' and they are based at 124, Broad Street, Ealing; that's just off the A40 I think," he said as he wrote the address, telephone number and email address on a yellow 'post it' note, which he handed across to Connelly. "If you do see him, say 'hello' to him from me, and ask him to pop in for a coffee sometime and a catch up," the Major said, before standing up.

"Will do Sir, and thanks for your help. Now I'm back in circulation, I will be popping in myself on a pretty regular basis again, in case you need anything from me on the IT side," Connelly replied, getting up himself and shaking the Major's hand, before leaving the office and going out into the late morning sunshine.

As soon as he had left the Community Centre, Connelly took out his mobile phone, and called the telephone number the Major had written on the 'post it' note. After a few rings, his call was answered by what sounded like a mature, well-spoken lady, probably in her fifties or sixties Connelly guessed. "Good morning, Guards Security, can I help you?" the voice on the other end of the call enquired.

"Good morning, I would like to speak to Mr Cunningham if possible; it's Brian Connelly," the ex-Staff Sergeant replied. "Anthony knows me, and I might have a job for him."

"Just hold the line a moment Mr Connelly, and I will see if Mr Cunningham is free," the lady answered, and she was replaced with some nondescript background digital music for a short while, before coming back on the line. "Putting you through now Mr Connelly," and her voice was then replaced by that of the former army Captain.

"Good morning Brian, great to hear from you. How the hell are you?" the ex-Captain asked, then continued before Connelly had chance to answer, "Brenda says you might have a job for me?" and then paused, finally allowing the ex-Intelligence Corps man to respond.

"I'm fine thanks Tony, and yes, I might have something for you. Are you free this afternoon, or sometime tomorrow, for a meet?" Connelly asked.

"Can't make this afternoon Brian, something on, but I am free tomorrow morning after 10am. Do you want to come over to my office, or meet somewhere else?" Cunningham suggested.

"If it's all the same to you, I would rather make it away from your place. I will explain everything when I see you. How about meeting at the Vet's offices around 11am? I was there this morning, and it was Major Whyatt who gave me your details. Then, after our meeting, you can have a coffee and catch up with him. I know he would be pleased to see you again."

"Okay, that's a date Brian. See you tomorrow morning." and the two men finished the call.

Connelly then went down into the Underground network, and returned to his apartment for some lunch, which would consist of a couple of homemade chicken salad sandwiches, with a banana and glass of orange cordial, before carrying out the last two jobs on his 'to do' list.

After finishing his lunch, he took out his laptop, and brought up copy files of the 'incursions' into his three residences. He edited out the three team leaders holding up the contact message and mobile number, plus any frames which he deemed unnecessary, or which showed things he preferred not to be seen. These were mainly shots of the complicated array of screens, computer towers and printers, which made up his IT network in the London apartment, and then copied all the remaining footage from the three residences onto a 32GB memory stick.

He then took out one of the new, unused PAYG phones he had recently bought, and called the contact number he had been given from the CCTV recording. The call was answered after a short pause, and the same South African voice greeted Connelly.

"Good afternoon Mr Connelly, very pleased you called back so soon," Andre Botha answered, and waited for the ex-Intelligence Corps man to speak.

"Hi, do I discuss the next steps with you?" Connelly asked, not sure how he was supposed to proceed.

"No, if you have sensibly decided to return the money to its rightful owner, then I am to arrange for you to contact the interested party directly yourself," the South African replied.

"In that case yes, I am happy to proceed along those lines. What is he proposing?" Connelly asked.

"He is quite happy for you to decide on the arrangements. Initially, he suggests you call him, on a secure line of course, and then you can come to a mutually acceptable arrangement to complete your business."

"That's fine by me," Connelly replied. "It will take me several weeks at least to get the money together, as it is invested in several different areas around the world and, as you will appreciate, you cannot just ask to cash several million pounds of investments overnight. Give me the contact number, and tell our mutual friend I will get back to him, as soon as I am in a position to conclude our business."

"Will do," Botha replied, and after dictating the contact mobile number to Connelly, the South African ended the call.

With that, Connelly had completed his day's work and, as he could not do any more until the following day, when he would meet up with ex-Captain Cunningham, he decided to go out later to one of his favourite local restaurants, and have a pleasant relaxing evening.

Chapter 13

The PAYG phone in Underwood's desk 'pinged', announcing an incoming message just before 2pm in the afternoon, shortly after he had returned from a meeting in downtown Dubai. The exiled solicitor opened the top drawer of his desk, and took out the PAYG iPhone with the number '1' in a small circle in the top right-hand corner of the 'message' icon on the phone's display. As that mobile number was only used by one particular person, Underwood immediately took out the phone and accessed the message. It read "Target has made contact and is willing to return the goods. Please ring asap to discuss." He then accessed the one number in the phone's directory and called the South African.

The solicitor's call was answered on the third ring. "Good afternoon Jonathon, thank you for calling so promptly," Andre Botha greeted him cheerily.

"Good afternoon Andre, what have you got for me?" Underwood asked eagerly.

"Connelly has been back in touch and, as anticipated, he agrees to return the money, but is asking for time to retrieve it from the various locations where he says it is invested. He says it will take several weeks, and then you can discuss how and where to complete the transaction. I have given him your contact number as instructed," Botha informed him.

"As I expected, he is buying some time in order to investigate his options, no doubt," Underwood replied. "The delay is fine with me, but at least he is sensibly agreeing to my proposals. Ultimately, he knows he will have to return whatever cash we decide will be acceptable to us both, whilst I am sure he will also be putting together some sort of information package regarding me, to be published should something untoward happen to him, as security for his wellbeing, after he returns my money," Underwood added, and then he continued after a short pause. "On to another matter Andre, which has been on my mind for quite a while. I have decided to try and arrange a meeting with my wife, Abigail. I have not contacted her since my disappearance, as the police were undoubtably monitoring her phones, emails, and social media. I know it could be potentially dangerous for me, but I have decided she deserves some sort of explanation. We can also discuss what she would like to do regarding our marriage, whether she would consider coming out here for a new life together, or if she would prefer to sever all ties and start a new life where she is."

"How do you propose to organise that, Jonathon?" Andre asked, knowing that to pursue that course of action would undoubtably put his client at risk.

"Initially, I need you to get a message to her Andre, through one of your operatives, preferably face to face somehow, in case she is still being monitored electronically. Find out if she is open to the idea; she may refuse point blank and that would end it there and then. If she agrees, then the idea I have is that she could arrange a shopping trip with some of her girlfriends to Paris, and I would arrange to meet her somewhere there," suggested Underwood. "If she does agree, then your man can arrange to contact her, using new PAYG phones, to make the arrangements, and I could call her once she is in Paris and hopefully meet up with her for a chat before she returns to Cheshire. Obviously, there is a large element of risk involved, because she could agree to go ahead with the meeting and go straight to the police with the details, then they could monitor the phones and be waiting for me when we do meet up. I'm hoping she won't do that. I think she'll either refuse at the initial contact, in which case I'll take it that she wants a divorce and new life, or she will go ahead with the clandestine meeting. What do you think Andre?" Jonathon asked the South African anxiously.

"Like you said, I think it's very risky, but I also understand your reasons. I know you are very fond of Abigail, and it would be the right thing to do for her sake," Underwood's friend and business colleague of many years replied. "Leave it with me Jonathon, and I will get back to you as soon as possible."

"Thank you Andre, speak soon," and the solicitor ended the call.

....

It was ten days before Botha called Underwood back, to inform him of the result of his attempted contact with the solicitor's wife. A two-man team had been sent up to Alderley Edge in Cheshire, initially to track Abigail's movements for a couple of days, to confirm that no other interested parties, namely the police, were similarly carrying out surveillance on the missing solicitor's wife. Once they were happy that indeed they were the only ones interested in Abigail's movements, one of the two men went to her apartment door, five minutes after she had returned home alone from a Pilates session with two of her friends. The second man went across the road and stood outside a small bistro, seemingly to study the menu, which was fixed to the inside of the main window, next to the entrance. On arriving at her apartment door, Andre's man posted an envelope through the apartment's letterbox, rang the bell a couple of times, and then quickly disappeared down the flight of stairs and across the road to join his colleague, and then they both entered the bistro and sat at a table at the rear of the mainly empty eatery. The envelope they had delivered to Abigail contained a simple message typed on plain paper which said, "We have an urgent message for you regarding your future marital status. The two of us are sat in the bistro opposite. If you do not come in the next five minutes, we will presume you are not interested."

The two men were still looking at the menus, when Abigail walked through the bistro door three minutes later. She had a quick look around the restaurant before spotting the two men, who were both looking at her. She then walked over to them and nervously sat down on one of the two empty chairs at their table. The two men smiled at her reassuringly, and one of them spoke as soon as she was seated. "Thanks for coming Abigail," he said quietly as he passed a small piece of folded paper to her across the table. "We'll keep this brief if you don't mind. Please call this number at about 7pm tonight from a public phone box - there is one just down from the Nat West Bank on the High Street."

Abigail nodded, immediately picked up the note and put it into her small black leather clutch bag, before standing up again and going back out of the bistro, casting a last nervous glance over her right shoulder at the two men as she did.

As Abigail left, a young waitress in a smart black skirt and white blouse approached the two men and took their order, before disappearing back into the kitchen. Forty minutes later, the two men left the bistro, having enjoyed an excellent meal, and returned to their car, a black Audi A4 saloon, which was parked in a 'Pay and Display' carpark, behind the row of shops, pubs and restaurants on Alderley Edge's main thoroughfare, and waited for Abigail's call.

At five past seven, the PAYG mobile, being held by the man in the passenger seat of the Audi A4, vibrated to announce an incoming call. He answered it immediately, "Thanks for calling Abigail. Before we start, please can you tell me where you are calling from, and the phone's number," having made a note of the call box's number earlier.

"Yes, I am calling from the phone you suggested by the Nat West," she replied and then read out the number, which was printed on an information notice above the phone, and which corresponded to the one which the man had written down earlier.

"Excellent Abigail. Now please hang up and I'll call you back immediately, alright?"

"Okay," she replied and put the phone back down, as instructed.

Almost immediately the phone started ringing, and she picked it back up.

"Sorry about all that," the man apologised, "but we have to be careful, you understand."

"I understand, have you come from Jonathon?" Abigail asked anxiously, "I haven't heard from him since he disappeared."

"No, not from him directly, but we do have a message he wants relaying to you," he replied, but before he could continue Abigail broke in.

"Is Jonathon okay, can I speak to him or see him?" she asked quickly, holding back her tears.

"Yes, he's fine, everything is fine," the man answered, trying to calm her down. "That's what we are here to try and arrange, but you will appreciate we have to be very careful. The police are still searching for him and we have no doubt that you are still under surveillance, in case of any contact between the two of you."

"Yes, I understand that" Abigail replied, "Sorry."

"Nothing to apologise for Abigail, it must be very distressing for you." Then after a short pause the man continued. "Okay, so I take it you are happy to contact Jonathon, to discuss how you would like to move forward with your relationship," he paused again to allow Abigail to confirm that, which she duly did. "Your husband proposes that, if possible, he would like to meet up with you in person, when he will explain everything that has happened and ask you what you want to do in the future. Then you can decide whether you want to try and get back together somewhere safe for the both of you, or if you would prefer to cut all ties and carry on as you are without him," he continued as instructed by Andre Botha.

"Yes, I would like to arrange to meet Jonathon, if possible," Abigail answered immediately.

"Okay, good," he continued. "We suggest you organise a long weekend shopping trip to Paris with two or three of your friends, say Friday to Monday, as soon as you like. When you have made the arrangements, buy a PAYG phone and use it to text the dates you are going, and the hotel you are staying at, to the mobile number I gave you in the bistro. We will also use that new phone to contact you if we need to, before your trip, so leave it on at all times. When you get to Paris, buy a French PAYG phone as soon as you arrive, and text that number to us as well, and then you will be contacted sometime during your visit on that phone, to make arrangements to meet your husband. Have you got all that Abigail?"

"Yes, I think so," she replied hesitantly.

"Okay, don't worry. If you have any questions, text me on your new PAYG phone, and remember only to use that phone to contact us," and with that, they ended the call.

As soon as Abigail hung up, the Security Company operative took out another phone. Then, as instructed, immediately called the head of his company, Andre Botha, who was expecting the call and answered it at once.

"Yes?" Andre asked expectantly.

"She wants to go ahead with the Paris meeting. She seems genuine," the operative informed his boss.

"Excellent, and you think she will carry out our instructions and, hopefully, not go to the police?" Andre asked.

"Yes," came the one-word reply.

"Okay, well done. That's you two finished up there. See you back in the office tomorrow," and Andre ended the call.

Andre then selected one of the mobile phones on his desk, and sent a text to the only number in the directory, which read "She wants to meet and will arrange trip as discussed."

Chapter 14

Brian Connelly arrived at the Veterans Community Group offices the following day, but twenty minutes before his pre-arranged meeting with ex-Captain Anthony Cunningham, knowing that Cunningham would arrive exactly on time, and not wanting to arrive together in case someone had the Centre under surveillance. Connelly went straight through to Major Whyatt's office, after getting a cup of coffee from the vending machine in the Centre's entrance foyer. As usual, the Major was at his desk, and looked up surprised when Connelly came through the door. "Don't see you for a couple of months, and then you turn up two days running," the head of the Vet's Group said with a smile, "So, what can we do for you today?"

"I called Anthony Cunningham yesterday on the number you provided, and he is alive and well and very much open for business, Sir" Connelly replied. "I hope you don't mind, but he is coming in at 11am to discuss that job I mentioned to you I might have for him. It seemed a good place to come to have a chat, and then you can have a catch up with him afterwards, killing two birds with one stone."

"Good idea Brian; would you like to use my office for your meeting? I can go through to the Walk-in Centre, there's a couple of Vets who came in a little earlier, and I will see how they are getting on."

"I was going to ask if that would be okay, Sir. Thanks for offering, it will give us a little privacy, as it is quite a sensitive issue," replied Connelly.

"No problem Brian, I'll go through after I have said 'hello' to Cunningham". The two men then continued to chat about the comings and goings at the Vets Centre, until exactly at 11am, ex-Captain Anthony Cunningham walked through the open office door.

The Major was the first to stand and move towards Cunningham saying, "Good morning Tony, good to see you again," followed immediately by Connelly who repeated the greeting, and then both men shook the ex-Captain's hand firmly.

"I believe you and Brian have some business to discuss Tony, so I'll leave you to it. I'll be through in the Walk-in Centre if you need me, and Brian don't forget to say goodbye before you go. I'll see you after your meeting Tony, for a coffee and a catch up if you have time."

"Definitely, Sir," Cunningham replied, with Connelly nodding in silent agreement, before Major Whyatt left his office to the two former soldiers, closing the door behind him.

Connelly went round the desk and sat down in the Major's chair, and Cunningham sat in the one just vacated by the ex-Int Corps man.

"Thank you for coming in Tony," Connelly began, "but you know what us Intelligence chaps are like - everything is always a bit 'cloak and dagger'."

"No problem Brian, after all the help and IT equipment you gave me setting up the business, I am more than happy to help you in any way I can," replied the head of Guards Security & Investigations. "What is it you would like me to do for you?"

"It's in two parts really, and the second part is conditional on completing the first assignment," Connelly began.

"Sounds like an exam," joked Cunningham, interrupting his ex-Army colleague.

"It definitely isn't a written test Tony, and it potentially could be quite dangerous, so reserve your offer of help until I let you know what is involved," Connelly continued seriously.

"Sounds intriguing Brian, pray continue," replied the now very interested ex-Fusiliers officer, leaning forward in his chair.

"Before I start Tony, I want to reassure you that, although there are almost certainly criminal elements involved in this, nothing that I ask you to do will be of a criminal nature," Connelly paused, allowing Cunningham to comment if he so wished. When he remained silent, Connelly continued, "The first thing I would like you to do, is identify the company that carried out an illegal search of my three homes recently," as he withdrew the memory stick, onto which he had downloaded the CCTV footage, from his zipped jacket pocket and passed it across the table to the ex-Captain. "This contains copies of their visit, all three were carried out simultaneously at properties in London, Newcastle, and a house in the Cotswolds not far from Oxford. There are six people involved, and one of each of the three two-man teams has a body camera and microphone and headset, and appears to be giving a running commentary to a third party or parties as they search. This would indicate to me a large, well-equipped concern who, I am guessing, is probably an officially licensed, legitimate investigation company with an equally large 'off-the-books', illegal side to their business. I think they are probably based in London, or maybe Manchester, going off what I know about them and the person who I think is probably employing them. Before you ask, the Police are not involved, and hopefully will not be at any time in the future. As you may or may not know Tony, since I left the Service, I have dabbled, very successfully, in the stocks and money markets, plus a little in the bullion markets. I think that someone, and I have an idea of who it might be, organised the search to try to find out what I am currently working on, and planning to invest in, which involves quite a substantial amount of money," Connelly explained, going with the fictional storyline for the benefit of the man sat across from him. "If you can identify the company who was hired to do these searches through the recordings, and your local knowledge of the firms who would potentially fit my description, I would then like to know as much as possible about them, their history, and their personnel. If you are successful in doing that, then hopefully between us we will be able to confirm the identity of whoever is behind it, and then I can take whatever appropriate action I deem necessary. What do you think?"

After quite a lengthy pause, the ex-Fusiliers officer replied, "There aren't that many firms, with the personnel to commit six well-equipped operatives to that kind of simultaneous operation, along with their normal day-to-day business, even in London. There can't be more than half a dozen at most, and far less in Manchester I think, so it's not a big list to go at. Leave it with me, and I'll have a look at the CCTV, and get back to you as soon as I have anything Brian."

"Excellent Tony, I was hoping you would be up for it. Couple of things, firstly payment. I insist you charge me at your standard company rates and secondly, and more importantly, proceed with extreme caution. I don't know who this company is, but I am sure they could prove very dangerous, if they were to discover that you were looking into their illegal activities," Connelly concluded.

"Give me an email address, and I'll send you all our charges and payment options, along with a contract for you to sign engaging our services. That way, everything is all above board and official, just in case you need something from us during the investigation. As regards being careful, we always are old chap. It goes with the territory."

Connelly wrote one of his email addresses on a piece of paper he tore from his notepad, and handed it across to Cunningham, along with the number of one of his unused PAYG mobiles.

"If you need to contact me Tony, use that number. It will be on 24/7, but leave a message if I don't answer it immediately. Anything else?"

"No, I don't think so Brian. You off now?" Cunningham asked.

"Yes, I'll just nip through to say cheerio to Major Whyatt first, and then I'll be off." With that Connelly stood up, shook hands with the ex-Captain and went through to the Walk-in Centre, where he said his goodbyes to the head of the Vets Community Group, before leaving the Community Centre and returning to his apartment in the West End of London.

Chapter 15

Abigail sent the text which Andre Botha and her husband had been anxiously waiting for, two weeks after her meeting with two of Andre's operatives in Alderley Edge. She, and her two girlfriends, would be flying down to Heathrow Airport from Manchester, then catching a connecting British Airways flight to Paris Charles de Gaulle Airport a week on Friday, and staying at the Hotel La Comtesse on the Avenue de Tourville, until the following Monday. She would then fly back by the same route, arriving at Manchester early that Monday evening.

As soon as Andre received the message, he forwarded it to Jonathon in Dubai, who immediately responded with a 'thumbs up' emoji in acknowledgement.

The solicitor then went onto his laptop and 'Googled' the Hotel La Comtesse, before booking an hotel on the other side of the Seine River, but within reasonable walking distance of Abigail's, for the corresponding Sunday, Monday, and Tuesday. He then booked his return flights from Dubai to Paris, and called Andre to inform him of his plans and ask him for a favour.

When Andre answered his call, Jonathon told him of his plans and made his request.

"Andre, would it be possible for a couple of your best men, to come over to Paris for the couple of days before I arrive there, just in case Abigail brings some unwanted guests with her?" the solicitor asked.

"I was going to suggest the self-same thing, Jonathon. They could arrive around the same time as Abigail and see if anyone is tailing her - police from England, France, or possibly both," the South African replied.

"Exactly Andre, and if she is being followed, I can then decide what to do next," Jonathon agreed.

"We have advised her to buy a PAYG phone while she is over there, and let us know the number. We will then let you know it, and at least you will be able to contact her if she is being tailed, and you are unable to meet up face to face," Andre further advised him.

"Sounds like a plan Andre," Jonathon agreed. "Once I arrive, get your men to contact me on this number and give me a situation update, and then we can go from there." The two men then said their goodbyes and ended the call.

Chapter 16

Chief Superintendent Washbourne was sat at his desk when his Personal Assistant called through to him on the internal telephone.

"Sir, I have DI Greenwood on the phone for you."

"Put him through please," Washbourne replied and he immediately greeted the Detective Inspector with a cheery, "Good Afternoon Richard, what can I do for you?"

"We have turned something up in the Underwood case, which could be of interest. Are you free anytime this afternoon?" Greenwood asked.

"If you could come over now Richard that would be fine, I have nothing on at the moment."

"Will do Sir, see you shortly," the Detective said and they ended the call.

Ten minutes later Detective Inspector Greenwood was shown into Washbourne's office by the Chief Superintendent's Personal Assistant, who then left the two officers alone, closing the door behind herself.

"Okay Richard what have you got?" CS Washourne asked once the men had settled into their chairs.

"This could potentially prove quite interesting, Sir" Greenwood replied, taking out an A4 sheet of paper from the open buff folder he had placed on the desk in front of him.

"Underwood's wife Abigail has organised a long weekend in Paris, with two of her girlfriends in a couple of weeks' time, ostensibly a shopping expedition and to see the sights. It is something she has never done before, and again coming so soon after Radcliffe's death, it seems too much of a coincidence not to be connected. It would also fit in with your theory that Underwood is tying up some loose ends, and contacting his wife must be pretty much at the top of that list, especially as we suspect he has refrained from doing so since his disappearance," the Detective Inspector reported.

"Yes indeed, Richard. That is very interesting indeed," commented the Chief Superintendent.

"They are flying down to Heathrow a week on Friday," Greenwood informed his superior officer, referring to the typed sheet of paper "and then catching a connecting flight to Paris, where they are staying at the Hotel La Comtesse on the South Bank, before returning home on the following Monday. It could be just a girls' weekend away shopping, but it could also be Underwood setting up a meeting with his wife. If it is the latter, it could be our first, and probably best, opportunity to finally get our hands on the elusive solicitor," the Detective Inspector suggested excitedly.

After a short pause, Chief Superintendent Washbourne nodded and replied, "Yes, that sounds very possible Richard. How did you come by this information?"

"That's our only concern, Sir. Abigail has been openly talking about it on her social media platforms and through emails and texts to her friends, saying when and where she is going, and how much she is looking forward to it. She has not tried to hide the trip, so she is either being very clever by appearing so open about the arrangements, or it is what she is saying, simply a weekend away with her friends," DI Greenwood continued.

Again, there was a short pause while his senior officer considered this additional information, before he spoke again. "Yes, you are right Richard, it could be what it purports to be, a shopping weekend away, but coming at the same time as these other events, I definitely think it is worth following up. What do you suggest?" Washbourne asked, after making his decision.

"I think we should send a couple of Detectives over there for her visit, follow her wherever she goes and, if we get lucky, see if Underwood does meet up with her and finally get our hands on him. Obviously, we will need to contact the French and make arrangements with them; hopefully you can organise that Sir," he began, looking for confirmation from the Chief Superintendent, who immediately nodded in agreement. "I have a couple of officers in mind, Sir," Greenwood continued, "Detective Sergeant Foden from our team, and a Detective Sergeant Bury from the Drugs Squad, who speaks fluent French and knows Paris well, having been over there a few times on previous cases."

"Excellent Richard, I'll get everything signed off and arrange a contact for you over in France. Keep me updated as soon as you hear anything, and good luck; let's hope this is our first break in the case. Anything else for me?"

LOOSE ENDS

"No Sir, that is it for now," Greenwood replied before thanking his superior for taking the time to see him and then leaving the Chief Superintendent's office.

Chapter 17

Just under two weeks after receiving confirmation of Abigail's trip from Andre Botha, Jonathon Jones (formerly Underwood) disembarked at Paris Charles de Gaulle Airport after a very comfortable seven-hour fifteen minutes flight, which was five minutes early landing, on Emirates Airways.

After passing seamlessly through passport control and customs, Jonathon took a taxi to his hotel. He booked in and went straight to his room, which in fact was a two-room suite. The suite had a separate lounge area, a panoramic view over the river and also, in the distance, a view of the Eiffel Tower.

As soon as he had unpacked his suitcase, he took out his iPhone, and texted the number Andre had given him previously to contact his two Security Company's operatives, who had arrived in Paris two days earlier. The message read, "Just arrived at hotel. Please update."

"Can confirm that 'A' has three 'tails'. One French and two English. What is your room number? Will come over to you in one hour for full report," came the quick reply.

Jonathon acknowledged the message giving them his room number, and then picked up the room telephone, called room service and ordered some sandwiches and a large pot of coffee, for delivery as soon as possible. The fact that Abigail was being watched disappointed him, but he was not surprised, as he knew how determined the forces of law and order were to apprehend him. He started to have second thoughts about coming to Paris, but then he dismissed them almost at once. He deeply regretted having to leave England without a word of explanation to his beloved wife, but he knew it had been the best course of action for both of them in the long run. However, he was determined to rectify that situation, explain his motives, and offer Abigail whatever solution she decided to make regarding their future together, if there was to be one.

The knock on his hotel room door came fifty-five minutes after he had received the text, and Jonathon went over to the door, looked through the small 'spy hole', and seeing two casually dressed men, opened the door and signalled them to enter, closing the door after them.

"Good afternoon, Mr Jones," the taller of the two men spoke first. "My name is Dan and this is Philippe. He speaks fluent French and was a native of Paris, before moving to the UK fifteen years ago, which has been a great help," Dan added smiling, and his French speaking colleague nodded in acknowledgement.

"Can I get you anything from room service gentlemen, before we start," asked the solicitor, as he motioned for the two men to sit down on chairs in the adjoining lounge area of his suite.

"No thanks, we are fine," Dan replied, looking at what remained of the plate of sandwiches and coffee, which were on a small side-table against the wall.

"Okay," Jonathon said, walking over to the large bay window and turning to face the two men, keen to get a full report from the operatives. "You said that Abi is being followed."

"Yes, there are three police tailing her. Two English detectives, one male and one female, and a French officer from the Gendarmerie, who no doubt will be acting as guide, interpreter, and liaison between the two forces. Like us, they picked Abigail up at Charles de Gaulle, and have been following her very discretely ever since. Shortly after she checked in at her hotel, we saw the French officer go up to the receptionist, show her his badge and have quite a long conversation with her, before leaving one of his cards. Philippe managed to get quite close to them for some of the discussion, and he thinks he was asking her and any other reception staff to let him know immediately if Abigail, the lady who had just checked in, received any phone calls or anyone left any messages for her. He had reassured the receptionist the new guest was not involved in anything criminal, but she may unwittingly be involved in something they were investigating, and they were keeping a watchful eye on her for her own safety. He stressed that none of the staff should inform the guest of the police's interest in her, as that would alarm her and would undoubtedly ruin their wider operation. They have followed her everywhere she has been, to the shops, restaurants, and the bar they went to last night. They are very good, and we are sure Abigail does not have the slightest idea that she is being followed by them. Do you need us to do anything else?" Dan asked, concluding his report.

"Do you have a description of the three officers following Abigail?" Jonathon asked after a short pause.

"Better than that," Dan replied, "Philippe managed to take photographs of the three of them, when they were sat at an outside café table, across from the bistro where Abigail and her two friends were having lunch, after doing some shopping in the Latin Quarter. I'll get Philippe to copy them off his camera, and then text them across to you when we get back to our hotel."

"Brilliant, Dan. Thank you for that. You can return to London now and thank you for your help, unless you can think of anything else?" the solicitor asked.

"No, I think that is everything Mr Jones. Good luck," and with that, the solicitor showed them to the door, shook both their hands before thanking them once again, and finally closing the door behind them.

Jonathon went to the room's large and well stocked minibar, took out a bottle of premium lager and emptied it into one of the glasses, which were on the tray on an adjoining side-table.

Now that he knew that Abigail was under close surveillance, he had a dilemma. Did he still go ahead with trying to arrange a meeting, or did he just call her on the PAYG phone and have a conversation that way, which obviously would be the safest course of action. Also, if he did try to meet up, did he tell Abi about her three 'tails'? If he did, then she would certainly be upset, and probably start acting suspiciously and try to identify her followers. This would alert the police officers that they may have been spotted, or that Abi was getting outside help from someone, possibly himself. This would just increase their surveillance on her, and make it harder to make contact and meet up.

After a long deliberation, he finally decided on a course of action. Thirty minutes later, his phone 'pinged' to announce an incoming message. He immediately accessed the text, which contained three photographs, clearly showing two men and a woman sitting outside a café having, what looked like, a large cup of coffee each.

Chapter 18

Early Monday morning, the last day of Abigail's Paris trip, Jonathon Underwood sent a text to her newly acquired French PAYG mobile phone which read, "What are your plans for today?"

Abigail, who had been anxiously waiting for some sort of contact from her exiled husband, let out a short shriek of anticipation when she heard the phone 'ping', just as she was about to enter the shower, signalling an incoming message. She immediately accessed the text and replied, "Sight-seeing with the girls. Louvre first after breakfast, then onto the Eiffel Tower and lunch at 1:00pm at Le Jules Verne restaurant there, before returning to the hotel and finally the airport and home".

There was a short pause before the phone 'pinged' again. The new text read, "Can you make excuses to girls while at Louvre soon after arriving, perhaps say you want to return to hotel for something you have forgotten, or perhaps to revisit one of the shops you have been to earlier? Tell them you will meet them at the Eiffel Tower for lunch as arranged. I will meet you at the Tower about 12 o'clock, at the Madame Brasserie restaurant on the first floor. Take a table and I will join you shortly afterwards. Use one of the side exits from the Louvre, not the main one you entered by, and get a taxi to the Tower. See you later".

Shaking with suppressed excitement, at the possibility of finally meeting up with her husband again after more than two years enforced separation, Abigail texted back the single 'thumbs up' emoji followed by two 'XXs'.

On receiving Abigail's reply, Jonathon relaxed back into the comfortable armchair in his suite's lounge, and looked out over the panoramic view of Paris and towards the Eiffel Tower in the distance.

....

An hour later, the solicitor was sitting at a window table in a café directly across the road from the main entrance to the Louvre Museum, slowly drinking a large cappuccino coffee. Jonathon was hoping that, as Abigail's trip was coming to an end, and she appeared to be making sight-seeing with her girlfriends the last thing on their itinerary before returning home, the three watchers would relax their surveillance, presuming that indeed Abigail's trip was exactly what it appeared to be, a shopping and sight-seeing weekend with her friends.

Forty minutes later, and on his second cup of coffee, Jonathon saw his wife and her two companions get out of a taxi and enter the Louvre's main entrance. Shortly afterwards, a blue Citroen pulled up and stopped at the same place as the now disappearing taxi, and the male and female English detectives got out and followed the three young women up the steps into the grand entrance to the Museum. The two detectives returned to the waiting Citroen shortly afterwards, and got back into the rear of the car before driving off. Jonathon, seeing the detectives leave, perhaps to find somewhere to park or, more hopefully, to leave the girls, thinking that Abigail was just going to spend an hour or so at the Museum, seized his opportunity and immediately sent a text to Abigail which read, "Slight change of plans. Bringing our meeting forward. Make your excuses in fifteen minutes and will meet you there as arranged", thus giving him time to arrive at the Tower before her.

Abigail read the text and, as she had previously decided she would, after looking at a couple of the exhibits, she told her two friends that she had a really bad headache, and needed to return to the hotel for some tablets and a lie down, and that she would join them later at the Tower for lunch as arranged. She then left the Museum by the rear entrance, hailed a passing taxi, and set off for the Eiffel Tower, just as Jonathon was arriving there.

Jonathon watched Abigail leave her taxi at the official 'dropping off' point for the Tower entrance, and then saw her walk through the foyer towards the lifts. The solicitor remained where he was for fifteen minutes watching for the blue Citroen, and possibly the appearance of the three detectives who were following his wife, from that or a different vehicle. When Jonathon had satisfied himself that Abigail had indeed eluded her watchers, he took a lift to the first floor and walked slowly into the Madame Brasserie, scanning the restaurant as he did, looking for his wife and confirming that none of the three detectives were also present.

As it was still an hour before the busiest time for the restaurant, there were still a few empty tables in the large eatery, but it took the solicitor a good fifteen seconds to locate his wife, who, although she had been watching, had not recognised her husband's entrance as he followed closely behind a young couple, whilst reassuring himself that the detectives were definitely not present in the restaurant. Seeing her, he then changed direction and walked between the occupied tables towards Abigail, who looked intently at him as he approached her. Jonathon was only a couple of metres from her before she finally recognised him as he took his glasses off, and she immediately stood up and the couple embraced warmly. Abigail was crying silent tears when they finally separated, and sat down next to each other at Abigail's table holding hands, neither wanting to lose touch with the other after such a long, enforced time apart. They just sat looking at each other, not able to speak initially, although both had so much to say and ask. Finally, still holding hands, it was Abigail who spoke first, "You are looking very well Jonathon."

"Thank you, Abi, and you are as beautiful as ever," her husband replied. Then there was another short silence before Jonathon spoke again. "Unfortunately, we don't have a lot of time, so please bear with me for the moment and let me say what I need to say. Firstly, and most importantly, words cannot express my regret for what has happened, and the sorrow my actions must have caused you. Yes, I have deceived you and yes, I did lead a criminal double life, but I have always loved you and foolishly believed I could get away with it, while providing you with the best life I could." Jonathon held up his hand in restraint as he could see that Abigail was about to say something. "Please hear me out Abi before you speak," and he continued. "I cannot undo what I have done, but I can offer you a couple of alternatives moving forward, and I will honour your decision, whichever path you decide to take. As you will have deduced from the lurid reports of my exploits in the papers and on social media, some of which are true and some vastly exaggerated, I am a very wealthy man, but I am now obliged to live the rest of my life hidden in exile. I can offer you two futures, one with me in my new home, or together in a different, equally safe haven of your choice. Or if you prefer to remain at home and continue as you are, then I will not try to dissuade you, and I will leave you in peace. You can easily get a divorce because I have been absent for more than the period required by law. We can keep in touch if you want, albeit exercising the upmost care whilst doing so, and I will ensure you are always financially secure. Obviously, you don't have to decide now, take as long as you want Abigail and then let me know. Use a new PAYG phone, and text your answer to that number my colleague gave you in order to arrange this trip."

Jonathon then glanced at his watch to check the time. "It's only five to twelve, so we still have forty minutes or so before you need to go up to the restaurant to meet your friends," he said, still holding his wife's hand. "Do you want a coffee or something?" he asked.

After a short pause she nodded, saying, "Yes, that would be nice Jonathon," and her husband signalled to one of the waitresses, who changed direction, approached their table, and took their order. Most of the next three-quarters of an hour's conversation consisted of Abigail bringing her husband up to date on her life since his enforced exile, and Jonathon politely refusing to inform his wife of his current life and new country of residence. He explained at length, if she was to be questioned by the police at any time in the future she could honestly answer that she was unaware of where he had disappeared to. It was not, as he was at pains to explain, that he did not trust her, but that it meant she could answer their questions honestly and truthfully.

Finally, and with great reluctance and a long, warm embrace, they parted company, Abigail promising that she would get back in touch with him as soon as she made her decision, one way or the other. As Abigail went over to the stairs leading to the restaurant above and Jonathon to the ones leading back down to the Tower's entrance, the thought struck him that this might well be the last time he would see his beloved wife, and he was filled with a terrible sadness and a growing, burning anger towards the men who had caused this turn of events.

Abigail walked into the Le Jules Verne restaurant at five to one, to see her two friends already seated at their table, next to one of the many large windows that looked out over the city.

"Are you feeling better Abi?" one of her friends asked.

"Yes thanks, much better. Have you ordered?" Abigail enquired as she sat down at their table.

"Not yet, we've looked at the menu, but thought we would wait for you," her other friend said in reply, and passed Abigail one of the menus that were lying on the table.

While Abigail was meeting with her two friends at the restaurant, Jonathon was sat on one of the many benches in the area outside the Tower entrance, with a large, unfolded tourist map of Paris in front of his face, appearing to study it, whilst keeping an eye on the people entering and leaving the famous tourist destination. At 1:05pm, he saw the three detectives walk up to the Tower entrance and head over to the lifts. Jonathon smiled as he folded the map back up again, stood up and walked over to the nearest taxi rank, where he got a cab back to his hotel.

Chapter 19

Connelly did not have long to wait, before ex-Captain Cunningham got back to him with his first update, regarding the investigation into who carried out the searches of his three residences.

Cunningham called him the very next morning after they had met at the Veteran's Community Group's offices in Lewisham, while the ex-Intelligence Corps man was just finishing, which for him, was a late breakfast.

"Good morning, Brian," Cunningham greeted his fellow ex-serviceman. "Hope I'm not interrupting anything?"

"No Tony, not at all, that was quick. What have you got for me?" Connelly asked immediately.

"Well, I have to admit, it has probably been the easiest assignment I have ever had. In fact, I am almost too embarrassed to accept payment for it - almost," Cunningham joked.

"What do you mean?" asked a very surprised Connelly.

"To quote an oft-used cliché Brian, do you want the good news or the bad news first?" Cunningham continued.

"The good news, please," a now intrigued Connelly answered.

"The good news is that I have identified the company whose personnel visited your three properties in the early hours of the morning," Cunningham began.

"That indeed is incredibly quick Tony, and the bad news?" Connelly asked slowly.

"The bad news is, that they would be in a list of my top two of companies I would not want to get involved with, and in fact, they would be my number one in that category," stated the ex-Army officer.

After a short pause, an alarmed Brian Connelly spoke again, "Details, Tony?"

"As I said Brian, identifying the company was extremely easy. From the information you gave me, firstly I compiled a list of companies in London who fitted the description you gave me; there were five of them. Then I watched the videos, taken at your properties of the three teams of two entering the said properties. I immediately recognised the team leader with the bodycam, microphone, and headset from the incursion into your London apartment. Even though he was wearing a ski mask, I would know that tall, wiry body and the smooth way he moves anywhere. It is Peter Stokes, an ex-Para. He was one of the Vets from the Community Group who helped me set up 'Guards' in the first place. He left me about twelve months ago to join this company for, what he told me, was double the money and, what he described at the time, as more 'interesting and varied' work, without going into any detail. I have since found out, through my contacts in the 'business', that the work he was referring to is mainly illegal, and completely off their legitimate and very successful security business books."

"And the company is?" asked an increasingly concerned Connelly.

"The company is called 'Security Contractors (London) Limited', and is based here in London. The guy who runs it is not a native of our shores and, as part two of your assignment was to discover the company's background, I have done quite a bit of research regarding this particular gentleman."

At this, Connelly visibly became more concentrated on what Tony Cunningham was saying, as he sensed that what he was about to hear, could help him immeasurably in his search for Underwood. Connelly straightened his back, sat very upright and then leaned slightly forward, before speaking into his phone, "Do go on, Tony."

"The head of the company is a South African called Andre Botha," Cunningham began, "who was a senior officer and young 'high flyer' in the South African Police, during F. W. de Klerk's presidency. I also think that he may be a distant relation of the previous President P. W. Botha, but I would need to dig further to confirm that one way or the other, as it is a pretty common name in South African. Then when Nelson Mandela became President, he, along with some of his fellow police officers, left and migrated to Dubai. They then set up a security company there, with Andre as their Managing Director, perhaps with the help of his people back home - I don't know for sure. Their main work was in 'Close Security' for a couple of the Sheiks, who were distant relations of the Crown Prince, and hence only minor Royals. However, their business grew through referrals within the very large extended Royal Family - all quite above board and legitimate. As their reputation grew, Andre's company's responsibilities also increased, and began to include accompanying their respective Sheiks over to England for the Flat Racing Season, something the Crown Prince and most of the Royal Family do each year. The Sheiks go to the racing, mainly Newmarket where they have a large presence, including their premier Stud Farm and some large estates, and their wives and daughters go on a shopping spree, at all the top designer and fashion boutiques in the West End. Apparently, after several very successful years in Dubai, Botha moved his main business and head office to London, where he continued to supply staff to the minor Royals on their England trips, in addition to taking on more new business here in London and the surrounding Counties. The Crown Prince and his close family, as you would expect, have their own dedicated people to supply all their needs; some they bring with them, and some are based at one of their own companies here in London. Again, all Botha's initial business here in London was both very successful and completely legitimate, fully licensed and approved by the authorities. However, talking to a few of my contacts within our business, and from things my operatives have picked up during various assignments, it appears that a few years ago, and completely without the knowledge of his high profile Arab customers, Andre branched out to provide additional 'off the books' services to certain other, carefully vetted, customers. These additional services basically include anything you want provided, almost exclusively illegal, for which you are prepared to pay a very high additional premium. Again, rumour has it, he has employed personnel who are especially adept at these more extreme measures. The operatives used, are mainly from the ex-Special Forces vets who have fallen on hard times, or people like Peter

Stokes. Peter had a reasonable job with us, and he is an ex-Para who is happy to take on the work which he was trained to do, for a much larger pay packet. I would imagine it would be an easy sell to a lot of these men, having been trained to such a high degree; then having been discarded by the Army, or having become disillusioned with the political system that employed them, and on leaving the Forces, receiving no, or very little, help to repatriate them back into civilian life. Many of them ending up on the street homeless, with drink and drug-related problems. I am afraid to report Brian, it is these men who are looking into your business, and as I said at the beginning, they are completely ruthless, and the fact that you are an ex-Serviceman yourself will mean nothing to them; you are simply a nominated target. Hopefully, they have only been employed to gather whatever information they were looking for, and nothing more," concluded Cunningham.

After a short pause Connelly finally replied, "Well, that's food for thought indeed, Tony. Please put together a full report, and I'll pick it up from you sometime soon at the Community Centre. Leave this with me for now, and I'll get back to you if I need anything else," he said, and with that Connelly ended the call.

"Well, that might explain a lot," Connelly said aloud to himself. "Dubai, not unsurprising," he continued, rationalising the information he had just been given. The UAE had been high on his list of potential destinations for the disappearing solicitor. "Let's see what we can find," he said aloud finally to himself, opening his laptop and 'booting' it up as he spoke.

He thought for a minute, and when the 'Google' page finally appeared on his laptop screen, he typed "New solicitor practices in Dubai" into the search engine, and tapped the 'return' key. The page instantly downloaded a host of different links to information answering his query, one of which listed a number of Dubai-based legal firms. Connelly scrolled down the extended list, and stopped midway through his search at 'JTJ Solicitors of Dubai'. He immediately recognised that JTJ were the initials of Underwood's birth name, knowing that he had changed his surname from Jones to Underwood while at university, from his earlier dealings with his then partner, Chief Superintendent Jonny Radcliffe, and the Manchester solicitor. It would appear he had changed it back for his domicile in Dubai.

He quickly clicked on the company's link, and was immediately taken to the solicitor's 'landing page'. There was only a brief biography, describing that he was in fact a sole practitioner, despite the plural form in the firm's title, providing legal advice and services relating to English Law, for citizens of Dubai visiting the UK for pleasure or business purposes. And, more importantly, there were no photographs of the aforementioned solicitor, which in itself was very unusual for normally self-publicity-seeking professionals. Connelly wrote the company name, address, contact numbers and their email address in his notebook, and then turned his laptop off, before picking up his mobile and calling Tony Cunningham back.

"Hello Brian," came the prompt reply, "I did not expect to hear from you so soon."

"Thanks to your excellent work Tony, I have another job for you," Connelly said. "How do you fancy a quick trip to Dubai for me?" the ex-Intelligence Corps man asked, "and before you ask, it has nothing to do with the South African or his company, legal or criminal."

"Well, that's a relief," Cunningham answered gratefully. "What do you want me to do?"

"I will text you the name, office address and contact details of a solicitor, who I think may be involved in hiring Botha's company to break into my homes," Connelly replied. "What I would like you to do, is take some pictures of him, ideally coming out of his office building, and then send them to me as soon as you can. Obviously, it is imperative that he has no idea that you are photographing him, so don't take any chances whatsoever. I don't need a close-up shot, use a telephoto lens if necessary, as long as he and the building are both recognisable. If you do that successfully, I can promise you a very large bonus on top of your standard charges, and any expenses you incur for the Dubai trip," he concluded.

"No problem, Brian. When do you want the photos by?" Cunningham asked happily.

"ASAP Tony," came the quick reply.

"Okay, leave it with me," Cunningham answered, "and I'll book my tickets this afternoon on the earliest available flight," and then they said their goodbyes and ended the call.

Chapter 20

Brian Connelly received the photographs from Dubai, the ones he was anxiously waiting for, ten days after issuing his request to the head of Guards Security & Investigations Limited. There were three of them, all obviously taken from a good distance away using a very powerful, high quality telephoto lens. There was one of a suited businessman, carrying a black leather briefcase walking into a multi-storey office block, with the name of the building clearly displayed above the entrance. One with the same man, carrying the same black leather briefcase, in the act of leaving the same building. And finally, one of him dressed in casual, beige-coloured trousers, a white open-necked short-sleeved cotton shirt and beige loafers, relaxed and sitting at an outside table of a café in a pedestrianised precinct, enjoying a long, iced drink of some description. The man in question was of medium height and build, tanned and healthy looking. He had a full dark beard and moustache, very short dark, almost shaved, hair and wearing a pair of silver, designer-framed spectacles. Connelly was very impressed with Jonathon's 'disguise'. The hair, beard and glasses made him almost unrecognisable, from the man he knew from a couple of years ago back in England. He also noted the solicitor had lost weight and was looking very fit.

The ex-Intelligence Corps Staff Sergeant looked at the three photos for quite a time, whilst he decided his next course of action. He knew he was going to have to return a large amount of the money to Underwood at some point, if he was to retain his good health. He now had the information he needed, to convince the solicitor to play by his rules after the handover. It was not a cast-iron guarantee, but at least it gave him a good chance to walk away from this with the remainder of his fortune, about fifteen million pounds, and his life intact.

Again, he took his time deciding his next move. It was imperative that he did not appear to be a direct threat to Underwood, or probably more especially Andre Botha, while he was alive, but at the same time, he had to show the solicitor, and the South African, that should anything fatal happen to himself after the money handover, then Connelly would be in possession of enough information to make life very difficult for both Underwood and Botha, by potentially posthumously publishing, through various media and online outlets, what he knew about both men.

Connelly finally took out the new, unused PAYG phone and sent a text to the number that Andre Botha had given him. It simply informed the South African that he had organised the monies, was ready to talk to Underwood, and asked him to get the solicitor to call him on this number to discuss the details. He paused for a moment before he pressed the 'Send' icon, knowing that he was far from sure he would come out of this in one piece, but after a further short interval, he took a deep breath and sent the text.

He received a reply almost instantly, informing him that Botha would pass the message onto Underwood, thanked him for his co-operation and said 'Goodbye', as he did not expect to have any further contact with Connelly.

The South African immediately forwarded Connelly's text to Jonathon, and wished him 'Good Luck', telling him if he needed anything further, to give him a call.

One hour later, Andre received a reply from Jonathon thanking him for his help, and asking the South African to let him know the bill to date for his services, which he would settle immediately.

Jonathon, who was sat at his office desk in Dubai, then took out another locally activated PAYG mobile in order to ring Connelly, before immediately putting it back in the drawer. If he rang the ex-Intelligence Corps IT specialist from his office, even on a PAYG phone, he was pretty sure that Connelly would have some sort of tracking device on the mobile phone he had been given to contact him on, thus giving away where Underwood now was, and that, he thought wryly, would not be a good idea. Instead, he decided he would ask Andre to get back to Connelly and tell him he would be in contact shortly, giving him chance to organise a quick trip back to Paris, from where he had recently returned, and phoning him from there.

He was still thinking about how he could organise that, when his office landline phone rang, showing on the display that it was from an international caller. Wondering who it might be, he picked up the handset and answered it himself, having dispensed with the services of a receptionist six months previously. "Good afternoon, JTJ Solicitors," he said, and waited for the caller to identify themself.

"Good afternoon Jonathon, it's Brian Connelly. I hope you are well. I thought it would be best if I just called you directly to sort all this out," the ex-Intelligence Corps serviceman said.

There then followed a stunned silence from the exiled solicitor, before he finally answered. "I suppose I should not be surprised, considering how highly your recently deceased partner spoke of you."

"Thank you Jonathon, I will take that as a compliment. And talking of compliments, your man Andre Botha is very accomplished at discovering one's whereabouts as well," Connelly added, wanting to show Underwood how much he knew about the solicitor's criminal network.

"You have been busy Brian. I suppose that puts us on a reasonable par, knowledge and information-wise, with each other," Underwood acknowledged.

"Exactly, it would not be in either party's interest to think about taking reprisals, once our business is completed. We both have too much to lose," Connelly agreed. "Now, on to the matter at hand," he continued. "I transferred just under nine million of your hard earned cash Jonathon, under instructions from my ex-partner, into his accounts and I propose to transfer that plus interest, totalling eleven million, back to you. What do you say?"

"Make it twelve million and we have a deal," replied the solicitor, after a brief pause.

"Twelve, and that's us straight, finished, yes?" Connelly asked, knowing that he had actually increased Underwood's money to fourteen million, with his astute dealings on the stock and money markets. He also had his own share from his partnership with Chief Superintendent Jonny Radcliffe, plus Radcliffe's even bigger pot, which he had also 'inherited' on the Chief Super's untimely death, making his own personal fortune from their criminal activity well in excess of fifteen million pounds, even after returning Underwood's money.

"It is indeed Brian. I will text you the three bank accounts I would like you to wire the money to, four million to each," the solicitor instructed him, not needing to take precautions now that he knew Connelly had his address and contact details. " Also, just a thought before you go. How do you fancy having a trip over here sometime before Christmas? As we are mutually dependent on each other, so to speak, for our continued freedom and good health, perhaps we could pool our resources and work together on some projects? I have no idea what at the moment, but I am sure it is something we could discuss at our leisure. What do you say?" Underwood asked tentatively, acting on the spur of the moment.

"I'll think about it, Jonathon. I am quite happy where I am and doing what I do, and I would prefer not to jeopardise it. But as I said, I'll give it some thought and get back to you. The money will be in your accounts by close of business tomorrow," Connelly advised him. "If there's nothing else, I'll say goodbye," he then said, wanting to finally end his connection with Underwood, at least for the moment, because he knew that he would never be completely safe from the solicitor, whatever assurances he was given.

"No, nothing at the moment Brian. But please give my proposal some thought, as I am certain it would be mutually beneficial," Underwood said before ending the call.

The following day, the twelve million pounds duly arrived in the nominated accounts, and Underwood sent a text to Connelly's mobile, "Monies arrived as instructed. Good doing business with you, and I hope to see you in the not too distant future."

Connelly received the text, smiling to himself and saying aloud, "I don't think so Jonathon", and promptly took the small sim card out of the PAYG phone. He then cut the card into four and deposited it in his waste bin. "Right," he continued to himself, "what's next?"

Chapter 21

Chief Superintendent Washbourne met with DI Richard Greenwood, on the day after the return of the two Met Police officers from their covert trip to Paris following Abigail Underwood in the hope that she had arranged to meet her missing husband, Jonathon. Washbourne knew that there had been no meeting, or at least not one the two assigned officers with their French colleague had observed, but he still wanted a first-hand report.

When DI Greenwood entered the Chief Superintendent's office at New Scotland Yard, he was accompanied by DS Foden who, along with DS Bury from the Drug Squad and an officer from the French police, had made up the small team following Underwood's wife. Washbourne signalled to the two detectives to sit down on the chairs opposite him, and once they were seated, he spoke.

"Good morning gentlemen. I know nothing came of your trip to Paris," he said, first looking at DS Foden, "but I would still like your report Foden, and then perhaps you Richard," he continued, switching his gaze to DI Greenwood, "you could update me on the rest of your team's work, and any possible future plans you might have regarding our attempts to locate our very elusive Manchester solicitor."

DS Foden opened his notebook and, after a quick scan through the few notes that he had made, confirmed to the Chief Superintendent that Abigail Underwood's trip to

Paris was, as far as his team had discovered, been exactly what it had been advertised as - a long weekend shopping and sightseeing with her friends. With the help of their French colleague, they had been able to keep a very close eye on Abigail, especially as she had booked all their main activities through the hotel's reception and concierge, who obligingly had passed all the details in advance to their French detective associate. Her mobile phone and emails had been monitored by the team back in London and, again, there was no suspicious traffic on them of any kind.

On the completion of Foden's report, the Chief Superintendent thanked him and then turned his attention to DI Greenwood.

"It was worth a try Richard, so what is next?" CS Washbourne asked, looking at the Detective Inspector.

"We will continue our electronic surveillance of Abigail and the McConnell brothers. I am sure they are still involved with Underwood somehow, and might lead us to him, and I can't believe he will not try and contact his wife at some stage - apparently they were very close. Apart from that Sir, we have nothing concrete to go on. We are still no nearer to discovering the identity of the mysterious IT man, and all the many millions of pounds that disappeared with him. On that Sir, have you had any luck with the Intelligence Corps people? I am convinced they could supply us with some very useful information regarding his possible identification."

"I am still working on that Richard. Hopefully I will get something useful back soon, but I cannot guarantee it."

After a brief pause, in case either of the two detectives wished to add anything, he continued, "If that's all gentlemen, I think we will call it a day for now. You never know, we could get a lucky break," the Chief Superintendent replied positively.

"I hope so Sir, we could certainly do with it," the Detective Inspector commented, before the two detectives left the Chief Superintendent's office, closing the door behind themselves.

Chapter 22

Ten days after returning to his new home in Dubai, after meeting his wife Abigail in Paris, Jonathon T Jones (formerly Underwood) was sat on his apartment balcony overlooking the sea, enjoying a large glass of chilled Pinot Grigio, when one of the two PAYG phones which were on the table beside him gave off a shrill ring, breaking his silent train of thought. Looking down at the offending phone, he immediately recognised it as the one whose number he had given to Abigail to contact him on, once she had come to a decision about their future life, either together or apart. He hesitated while the phone continued its piercing ring, shattering the peace of his previous quiet reflections, with a growing sense of dread as to the outcome of the forthcoming conversation. Eventually steeling himself, more in hope than expectation, he answered the call with a forced, light-hearted greeting.

"Good evening Abigail, how lovely to hear from you again. You are well I trust?" Jonathon asked.

"Yes thank you Jonathon," his wife replied, and from the nervous tremor in her voice Jonathon instantly knew what her answer was going to be, and he visibly shrunk in the chair and his shoulders slumped. "I am fine thank you," she quickly continued before her husband could speak again. "I have tried hard to convince myself that we could start and build a new life together wherever you are, and I have slept little during these past few days, but I am sorry my darling, I just cannot bring myself to leave everything I have built in the last couple of years, and live in hiding for the rest of my life, never knowing when the police might discover us, and then probably spending time in prison for however long. I'm sorry Jonathon, I just cannot do it," Abigail spoke, crying as she delivered her final decision to her husband.

After a long, silent pause, Jonathon finally replied to his wife. "I fully understand Abigail. I know it must have been very hard for you over the last couple of years and, as I promised you when we met in Paris, I will fully respect your decision, however much it pains me. Perhaps sometime in the future, if you would like to, we could meet up at various places and spend some time together," Jonathon suggested, already resigned to losing his beloved wife.

"Yes, perhaps Jonathon. I think I should go now," his wife said immediately ending the call, before bursting into a torrent of tears back in her apartment in Alderley Edge.

Jonathon just sat slumped, staring out over the balcony for what seemed like an eternity, before eventually sitting back up in the chair and picking up the other PAYG phone, having made a decision as to his next course of action. He accessed the only number in the phone's directory, and pressed the 'send' icon.

The phone was answered eventually in a deep South African accent, "Good afternoon Jonathon, what can I do for you," Andre Botha asked.

"Good Afternoon Andre, I hope you are well," the exiled solicitor replied. "I have decided on a new course of action, which could prove hazardous for both of us old friend, and that is I have decided to go after, and hopefully terminate, our IT 'friend' over in London. I will need your help, but obviously only if you agree because, as I said, it could lead to our exposure to the forces of law and order in the UK." Jonathon paused, waiting for a reaction from the South African, who eventually replied after a short silence.

"I presume you mean, the very strong possibility that he will have taken the precaution of leaving incriminating evidence regarding our illegal activities, to be publicised should anything happen to him?" suggested Andre.

"Exactly, so we need, or I should say you need, to try and find, if possible, where this evidence is, and nullify it before we take any actions against him," Jonathon agreed. "To that end, could I suggest you arrange a meeting with him over in London, and try and get a feel for the man, and at the same time find out everything you can about him; where he goes, who he meets etc, so we can build up a picture of him, and who he might trust with this potentially very incriminating information about us both."

"What has brought this change in direction of thought for you Jonathon? You could live out your life very comfortably and safely over there in Dubai if you wanted to, now that Connolly has returned your money," his South African confidante asked.

"True Andre, I have more than enough money now to live in quiet luxury for the rest of my life. But Abigail, quite understandably, has decided against joining me in a new life in exile. In addition, I can never return to my home in England as I would be forever looking over my shoulder. This, all because two greedy ex-partners decided to ruin an exciting business which I thoroughly enjoyed, and which could only have grown in size and diversity. We have gained retribution on the Chief Superintendent, but the other is living carefree in London, moving around doing whatever he pleases, enjoying his favourite pastimes, seemingly secure in the knowledge that he is beyond either capture by the police, or anything more serious from us. I am sorry Andre, but I'm afraid I cannot let that continue. We must find a way to make Connolly pay for the loss of my wife, my livelihood and my permanent exile in foreign lands."

"I understand what you are saying Jonathon, but as you quite rightly pointed out, this course of action carries many dangers for us, and could possibly land us in prison for a very long time," Andre replied. "Let me see what I can find out about Connolly, and I'll set up a meeting with him as you suggest. Once I have done that, we can talk again and see if your wish can be fulfilled. Please do not do anything rash before I get back to you." And with that, the two men said their goodbyes and ended the call.

Having started the ball rolling on his first and main objective, Jonathon then called three prestige real estate agencies in Dubai, and requested brochures on investment properties for sale in their area, telling each one he was looking at investing up to twenty-three million dirhams (five million pounds). He then arranged an appointment for the following week at his main bank in the city, to set up two trusts, each of the equivalent of another five million pounds each; one for his wife and one for his ex-friend and colleague Emrys Williams, for when he was released from prison in just under twelve months' time, having served half his allotted sentence. He knew the course of action he was embarking on was fraught with danger, and he could potentially end up in prison for a very long time, but he was determined to put as much of his financial affairs in order as possible in case of that unfortunate eventuality, and try and leave as much of a legacy as he could to the two people who he cared for the most. He would formalise everything in a new will under his assumed name here in Dubai, hopefully enabling them both to enjoy the proceeds of his criminal activities, without any interference from the UK authorities.

Chapter 23

The former Intelligence Corps Staff Sergeant sat down at the coffee table in his London apartment, with a notebook and pen in hand, determined to form a plan for resolving the very serious problem he had with how to deal with Jonathon T Underwood. It had been two weeks since he had transferred the twelve million pounds into the solicitor's overseas bank accounts, and no doubt the money had been immediately rewired to various accounts in different countries, before ending up who knows where. The money was not his concern, Underwood was welcome to it, and at least it had bought him some time; how much, he had no way of knowing. Connelly was certain that Underwood would be looking at ways, probably with the help of his South African henchman, to remove himself as a possible future threat to themselves, knowing what Connelly knew about their past criminal activities and the solicitor's new life in Dubai. As was his way, when trying to solve a problem, Connelly opened his notebook and, after a lengthy pause for consideration, set out his thoughts and proposed actions:

Objectives

1. Remove Underwood as a threat, preferably without involving Botha.
2. Assess possible alternatives for 1 above.
3. Compile digital evidence as insurance against Underwood.
4. Decide how/who to give 3 above to, for safe keeping.

5. Instruct 4 above who to pass on info to in 3 above, in event of his sudden demise.
6. How to manage all above without incriminating himself, leading to possible retribution from AB.

Actions

1. Firstly, as in 3, 4 and 5 above, compile all evidence relating to Underwood and Botha, including written outline of everything he knew about their criminal activities, plus copies of pictures and address details of Underwood in Dubai, and Botha's operatives' edited incursions into his three residences. Possible recipient Tony Cunningham?
2. Investigate possible use of Underwood's involvement in Belfast deaths, relating to his gemstone smuggling activities as answer to 1 and 2 above, using Irish as tools of revenge?
3. Or anonymous police tip-off regarding Underwood's new Dubai life as above?

After another lengthy period reviewing his notes, Connelly finally closed the notebook and took out his laptop, in order to complete his first task, putting together all the evidence he had relating to Underwood's criminal activities, his new Dubai residency and his involvement with Botha.

An hour later, having compiled a comprehensive dossier on Jonathon T Underwood, and copying it encrypted onto a 32GB memory stick complete with additional password protection, he put a call into ex-Captain Anthony Cunningham of Guards Security & Investigations Limited.

"Good morning Tony," Connelly greeted the ex-Army officer, who had answered the call after the second ring, "I hope you are well."

"Yes thank you Brian, what can I do for you?" Cunningham asked.

"I have another favour to ask of you, regarding your recent investigations on my behalf. Any chance we could meet up at the Vets' Centre this afternoon, say around three o'clock?"

"Yes, I could do that," he replied. "See you then," and the two ex-Army colleagues ended the call.

As before, Connelly arrived for the meeting thirty minutes before the arranged time at the Vets' Community Centre, and was chatting with a couple of ex-Army Vets in the Walk-in Centre, who were interested in joining one of his IT courses, when Tony Cunningham arrived at exactly 3pm. Seeing Cunningham arriving, Connelly excused himself from the two ex-soldiers, and walked over to meet him.

"Afternoon Tony," Connelly greeted him, "thanks for coming. The Major is out at the moment, and he said we could use his office if we wanted," he continued, as he led the ex-Fusiliers Captain through to the small office.

Connelly sat at the Major's chair, and Cunningham in one of the two chairs on the other side of the small desk. Once they were both seated, the ex-Intelligence Corps IT man took a small, sealed Jiffy bag out of his coat pocket, and passed it across to Cunningham.

"Inside there is a memory stick, Tony," Connelly said after a short silence, as Cunningham picked up the Jiffy bag. "It contains a comprehensive report regarding Andre Botha's company's illegal incursion into my three properties, and the man who I believe commissioned it and why - that's the man you photographed in Dubai. I have not mentioned your involvement in any of this. The memory stick is encrypted and password protected for extra security, and must only be used in the event of my sudden demise in the next few years, from whatever the apparent cause. The details of how to 'read' the information, plus your contact details, I will leave with my solicitors in a separate envelope attached to my will. As you said Tony, these men are completely ruthless. Hopefully, the steps I have now taken should conclude their interest in me, but this is just in case they decide otherwise."

"Understood Brian, I will put this somewhere very safe you can be sure. I presume they are not aware of my involvement in your affairs, or the recent investigation?" Cunningham asked.

"As sure as one can be Tony, other than perhaps our mutual involvement whilst originally setting up your business," Connelly confirmed.

"Anything else Brian?" Cunningham asked finally.

"No, that's it I think, and once again thank you for all your help. Please invoice me for an additional five thousand pounds to cover looking after the memory stick, and any further services you might be required to do in the future," Connelly added, before standing up and shaking Cunningham's hand.

"That's very generous Brian. Don't hesitate to give me a call if you need anything else," Cunningham replied and with that, the two men left the Vets' office and then out through two different exits from the Community Centre, into the London sunshine.

Once the ex-Intelligence Corps serviceman had returned to his London flat, he began to put his main, and probably only realistic, 'attack' strategy into action - trying to remove Underwood as a threat to himself. Connolly was convinced in his own mind that the solicitor would not let their apparent stand-off continue for too long; putting himself in Underwood's position, he knew that he would take the same course of action, that is to remove the threat to himself permanently. He had to try to make it look, as much as was humanly possible, that however Underwood met his fate, he was in no way involved, at least as far as Andre Botha might suspect.

His first call was to an ex-Intelligence Corps Captain, who he had served with in two of his three tours in Northern Ireland, and who he had kept in touch with after the Staff Sergeant had left the service. After passing the usual pleasantries, Connelly worked the conversation around to their service together during the 'Troubles', and whether the recently retired Captain had kept in touch with any of their colleagues and contacts from within the Belfast security forces. He used the pretext of planning a nostalgic trip back over there in the near future, and that he was keen to look up some of their old contacts and friends. After the ex-Captain promised he would email Connolly as many of their mutual colleagues' contact details from over in Northern Ireland as he could dig out, and agreeing to meet up sometime soon for a coffee and a chat, the two ex-Int Corps servicemen ended the call.

Just as Connelly was thinking what he should do for his evening meal, after doing everything he could for the moment to resolve his present predicament, his main mobile phone rang and 'Vets' Centre' appeared on the screen, identifying the caller's identity.

"Hello, Brian Connelly," he answered immediately.

"Hello yourself Brian, Major Whyatt at the Vets' Centre," the head of the Centre replied. "Sorry to bother you, but I've just had a visitor in looking for you, saying he might have some work for you. He said you had been recommended to him by a colleague who knew you from here, but that he did not have any contact details for you. He asked me for your number but I declined to give out personal information; however, I said I would pass on his details to you and that you would contact him if you were interested."

"And his name is, Sir?" asked the ex-Int Corps man, smiling.

"Yes, sorry Brian, the guy was called Andre Botha, and had a strong South African accent. He was well dressed, suit and tie, but I must admit he made me feel uncomfortable; he had an aggressive air about himself, if you know what I mean," Whyatt added. The Major then relayed the number the South African said he could be contacted on, and ended the call.

"I wonder what Mr Botha wants," Connolly said out loud, before entering the number into one of his new, unused PAYG phones, and pressing the 'send' icon.

The call was answered on the third ring; "Good evening Brian," the strongly accented South African voice greeted him. "Thank you for calling so promptly, I had tried the number we had for you previously, but it seems no longer to be in service," Botha added. When Connolly remained silent, Andre continued. "Jonathon thinks it would be advantageous if you and I could meet up somewhere in London, to discuss a possible future partnership between the two of you, as I think he mentioned during your last conversation. You could choose where and when of course." Andre paused again, this time waiting until Connolly replied.

After another short pause, Connolly obliged. "I don't see why not," he said, surprised that Andre had discovered his connection to the Vets' Centre, and what Botha's and Underwood's real intentions were, as he was certain that Underwood was no more interested in joining forces than he was. It also proved that he was obviously still a target of their further investigations, something which did not bode well for his future safety. "I'm free tomorrow afternoon around 3pm. How about we meet up at the café across from my flat, it's called 'Ron's Place'?"

"That's fine by me," the South African replied. "See you there," and the two men ended the call without any further pleasantries.

"Well, that was indeed unexpected," Connolly said to himself. "I wonder what he wants?" he continued thinking aloud. "If nothing else, it will be interesting to meet our Mr Botha; I shall look forward to it." And with that, he decided that he would eat out somewhere very expensive in order to celebrate what, in his mind, had been a very productive day.

Chapter 24

Having settled on his final course of action, which he knew could result in his capture and a lengthy prison term, if he was unable to stop Connolly providing the authorities with detailed evidence of his criminal past, Jonathon resolved to make the most of whatever time he might have, and enjoy it as best he could.

To that end, he decided on two main objectives . The first was to meet up with his wife Abigail once more, as it could be the last chance he would have the opportunity to spend some quality time with her if he was unable to ensure his continued freedom from capture and certain prosecution. The second was something that he had considered before, but had deemed it too risky. It was that he would dearly love to revisit the island of Anglesey, around where so much of his previously successful, and immensely enjoyable, criminal enterprise had been centred. On an impulse, he booted up his laptop and, once the 'Google' landing page appeared, he entered 'Plas Meirion,' Moelfre, Anglesey and then pressed the 'search' icon. Almost immediately, as he had hoped, a picture of the bungalow on Anglesey appeared, under the heading of 'Welsh Cottages to Let'. He knew that the bungalow, which he had originally used as the main drop off point for the smuggled gemstones from Nigeria, had been sold locally at auction by Wade Manufacturing Limited, one of the companies he had invested in as a 'silent partner' in the early days of his criminal activities. Wade's had been the previous owner of the property, and unwitting partner in that previously extremely lucrative enterprise, and he knew that it had then been placed by the new owner, whoever that was, onto the very popular Anglesey 'holiday let' marketplace. The solicitor had already been informed by his main employer, a minor Royal who was a distant cousin of the Crown Prince, that he was required to accompany the Sheik on a forthcoming business trip to London, something he had done several times before under his new identity without incident. The trip was scheduled in three weeks' time, and would probably last for a further three to four weeks whilst his employer looked at several properties in the Newmarket area, in the hope of buying at least one for his, and his family's, use during the annual Flat Racing Season. Underwood was confident his employer would allow him a few days' leave to visit his own 'family', so he checked the holiday bungalow's availability during those weeks, and was very happy to see that the property was free for the second week of the trip. He immediately booked the property in the name of Jonathon T Jones, using a credit card in the same name, and his Dubai office address, mobile and email contact details. He received confirmation of his booking shortly afterwards, followed by another email from Welsh Cottages which contained a full description of 'Plas Meirion'; its location, directions to travel to the property, what time it would be available from, when he would need to vacate the property at the end of the 'let', and how to retrieve the front door key from the 'key safe', which was sited beside the main entrance, around the side of the property facing the sea.

Having booked 'Plas Meirion', he then sent a text to his South African associate informing him of the dates of his impending trip to London, and asking Andre if he would let his wife Abigail know, and ask her if she would like to meet up with him. Andre acknowledged the message, and replied that he would get back to the solicitor with her answer as soon as possible.

Jonathon received a text from Andre three days later, informing him that, unfortunately, Abigail had regretfully declined his offer to meet up during his forthcoming trip, as she thought it to be too much of a risk to take. Her answer further strengthened his resolve to take his revenge on Connolly, whatever the risk to himself.

....

Three weeks later, Underwood was on board his employer's private jet, along with other members of the Sheik's close family and business entourage, enroute to the private airfield in the South of England, that was always used by members of the Royal Family for their UK trips.

They were all quickly ushered through customs and passport control, with only a cursory look at the group's paperwork and identification documentation, before being driven off in a small fleet of luxury Mercedes Benz saloons to their accommodation in a West End hotel, which was owned by the Royal Family through one of its many corporations.

Underwood had no difficulty in gaining the leave he required, and using one of the many luxurious saloons available to him, although declining the offer of a chauffeur for the trip, seven days after arriving anonymously in England. He left London via the A40 and M40, and was soon driving up the M6 on his way to North Wales, and his final destination of Moelfre, Anglesey.

He arrived at 'Plas Meirion', his rental property just outside Moelfre, shortly after 5pm, having set off seven and a half hours earlier. The journey had been relatively uneventful, and he had made three stops along the way at the services on the various motorways, to stretch his legs and have a bite to eat and a drink. He soon found the 'key safe' and using the five-digit passcode supplied by Welsh Cottages, he retrieved the front door key, took his two suitcases from the car boot, and entered the bungalow with a tingle of excitement, knowing how the cottage had played such an important role in his previously burgeoning criminal career. He quickly emptied his belongings into the two wardrobes and chest of drawers in the main bedroom, and his toiletries into the bathroom cabinet. Having taken a quick look around the property, he headed out of the back door and walked down the narrow winding pathway towards the sea, shortly afterwards joining the main Anglesey coastal path. He then turned right towards Moelfre, having checked his route on a large scale Ordinance Survey map of Anglesey before leaving the cottage, a map he had bought in London two days before his departure. As he walked towards his destination, he looked out over the bay, noting the several vessels of differing sizes and types which were anchored there, smiling to himself, wondering if any of them had originated in Nigeria and what their cargoes were, legal and illegal. Twenty minutes later, the exiled solicitor passed the RNLI Station, where the Moelfre Lifeboat was housed, on his left and then shortly afterwards the corresponding visitor centre, with the imposing statue at the front looking out over the sea, dedicated to Richard Evans, one of its famous Coxswains, on his right. He then turned the final corner on the coastal path, and the old fishing village of Moelfre opened up before him, and his ultimate destination 'The Kinmel Arms' straight ahead, directly overlooking the bay. He stopped for a moment to take in the view, before heading up to the pub and entering through the side door. It was just before 5:45pm when Underwood approached the bar and looked at the various options of beer, cider and lager that the pub supplied. He decided on one of the draught bitters, and when he ordered a pint the small, smartly dressed woman behind the bar asked him if he was intending to eat, which after a short pause he decided he would. After pouring his drink, she also supplied him with a menu, informing him that he could order his food at the bar any time after six o'clock, quoting his table number. He thanked her, and took his pint and the menu to the small four-seater table to the left of the two larger eight-seater ones, which were all positioned in front of the large bow window giving a panoramic view over the bay, and out towards Puffin Island, The Great Orme and Llandudno in the distance. He ordered his food shortly afterwards, and was soon enjoying the largest, and finest, portion of gammon, egg, pineapple ring, chips and salad he had ever had in a pub. After finally finishing his meal, he went back to the bar and ordered another pint of the same hand-pulled bitter, before sitting back at his table and slowly enjoying his drink, whilst looking out at the fabulous view over the bay, as the sun slowly set out towards the West and Ireland, out of sight, in the far distance. Just as he was thinking about leaving, two men, who were obviously good friends, entered the pub laughing together and went up to the bar. One of the men was quite distinctive looking, being slightly over six feet tall the solicitor guessed, well built, tanned and with a thick head of longish, white hair with a matching full beard.

"The usual John?" the barmaid asked, as the two men approached the bar.

"Yes please Fiona," the white haired man replied. "And a pint of that fizzy stuff for Steve as well, if it's not too much trouble," he joked, as his friend left him at the bar and sat next to the window, on one of the eight-seater tables facing the solicitor. The barmaid smiled, obviously knowing the two 'regulars' well, and pulled a pint of the same bitter that Underwood had bought, and then pulled a pint of one of the three lagers that were available, before placing them both on the bar top. After swiping his card in payment, the man picked up the two pints, placed them on their table and sat opposite his friend, with his back to Underwood. The two men both took a large, appreciative mouthful from their respective pints, whilst looking out over the bay in silence.

"Tremendous view," Underwood spoke, obviously aiming his statement at the two newcomers.

The white haired man twisted round in his seat, and looking at the tanned stranger who had a shaven head, full dark beard and black, thick rimmed glasses, replied, "Yes indeed, we never tire of it. John Wyn Thomas and this is Steve Guest. Are you down here on holiday?"

"Yes, I've rented a bungalow on the outskirts of the village for a few days," Underwood replied, instantly realising with a start that these were the two men who had initiated the original investigation into his criminal activities. He quickly recovered his composure, finished his drink and said his goodbyes to the two men before hurriedly leaving the pub.

"Seems like you put the wind up him John," his friend Steve joked, after the tanned man had left, before returning, as usual, to discussing their various ailments and the parlous state of the country and modern society in general.

After his chastening experience in 'The Kinmel Arms', Underwood kept as low a profile as possible while visiting the various parts of the island which had played a part in his criminal activities, including Red Wharf Bay, but definitely not 'The Ship Inn', after his scare at 'The Kinmel Arms'.

Underwood returned to London, after his very enjoyable and relaxing time on Anglesey, reliving his time as the head of a very successful criminal organisation, if only for a few days. There he continued his work, which involved processing all the legal papers associated with the purchase of the two properties the Sheik had decided to buy on the outskirts of Newmarket, before returning to Dubai two weeks later. The solicitor had only been back in his office a couple of days, when one of the PAYG phones in the top drawer of his desk started to ring and vibrate. He opened the drawer and took it out before answering, "Good afternoon Andre, and to what do I owe the pleasure of your call?" he asked with a smile.

Chapter 25

Before meeting Andre Botha the following afternoon, Connolly made an impromptu call into his long time solicitor's office, just before 11am. He did not have an appointment, but promising to only take up a few minutes of her time, and as they were long-time friends, he was ushered into her private office at 11:30am, at the conclusion of the solicitor's earlier meeting.

"Very good of you to see me Rachel," the ex-Int Corps man said, as he entered her office.

"Not at all Brian, please sit down," she replied, pointing at the chair on the other side of the desk from where she was sitting. "What can I do for you?"

Connolly took out two sealed brown envelopes from the inside pocket of the lightweight, three-quarter length rain coat he was wearing against the decidedly wet weather that London had been experiencing over the last few days. He handed them across to the solicitor as he spoke.

"The one with 'Will' written on the front, contains a few amendments and additions I would like added to my will please Rachel. The second envelope marked 'Private', is to be opened only by yourself on my death, and is separate from my will, from whatever cause. It contains some specific instructions to be carried out by a certain individual, whose name and contact details are contained within the document." Connolly paused, waiting for any reaction.

"Sounds all a bit cloak and daggerish, Brian. I hope you are not expecting anything untoward to happen, are you?" Rachel asked, trying to sound light hearted, but knowing Brian's background, half fearing something might be amiss.

"You know me Rachel, I like to play up to my Intelligence Corps background, but no, everything is fine," he replied, trying to allay any fears the solicitor may have regarding his cryptic instructions. "Again, thanks for seeing me at such short notice. Please don't get up, I'll see myself out," and with that, Connelly left her office, closing the door behind himself.

Connolly had a couple of hours to kill before his meeting with Andre Botha, so he returned to his flat. Once there, he opened his laptop to check his email 'Inbox', and smiled when he saw that at the top of the newly arrived emails was the one he was waiting for, from the ex-Int Corps Captain who he had served with in Northern Ireland. As promised, his former colleague had sent a comprehensive list of five other men they had known and served with in Belfast, including any contact details he still had for them, plus the same for three undercover contacts they had both used, who the ex-Captain thought were still operating there, as far as he knew. He hoped the information proved useful to Brian on his proposed trip, and he asked Brian to give his regards to any of them that he might meet up with. Connolly immediately sent a reply thanking the ex-Captain for his help, and promised to let him know the outcome of the trip, and suggested perhaps they should meet up on his return for a full catchup.

After making himself a late lunch of a slice of pizza with some oven-baked chips, washed down with a large mug of tea, Connolly relaxed for forty-five minutes before putting his rain coat back on. Then at 2:55pm, he wandered across the road to 'Ron's Place' for his meeting with Jonathon T Underwood's South African henchman.

Andre Botha was already sat at one of the tables at the far back corner of the café, sitting facing into the room with a full view of the café interior and entrance. He had not been there long, because he was still looking at the single page menu, with a young waitress stood patiently beside him, with her notebook and pencil in hand waiting for his order.

Botha saw Connolly enter the café and waved to him, signalling for him to join him, and at the same time politely asking the waitress to come back in a couple of minutes, when she could then take both his and his guest's orders.

As Connolly approached the South African, passing the waitress who was walking in the opposite direction, Botha stood up from his chair and extended his right hand towards him, "So good to finally meet you Brian," he greeted the ex-Int Corps serviceman with a broad smile and firm handshake. "Please sit down," he continued, pointing with his left hand to the other chair at the small bistro table. Brian returned the smile, and a slightly firmer handshake, which did not go unnoticed by the South African, before sitting down himself.

Still smiling, Brian spoke quietly to Botha, although there was no-one in their vicinity who might inadvertently overhear any conversation the two men might have. "I wish I was as equally pleased to see you Mr Botha, but I must admit I fail to see any reason for this meeting."

"Please call me Andre, Brian. As I said on the phone, our mutual acquaintance asked me to explore the possibility of you two joining forces, so to speak, and if you are interested, to arrange a face-to-face meeting between the two of you to discuss a potential partnership," the South African replied.

As the waitress returned to their table, the two men stopped their discussion and ordered a couple of large Cappuccino coffees, and remained silent until she returned with their drinks. Once she had retreated to the front of the café, Brian took up the conversation again.

"I am very sorry you have wasted your time Mr Botha," Connolly answered, pointedly continuing to use the South African's surname. "I thought I had made it clear to your colleague that, as far as I was concerned, our business was finished on the transfer of the funds, and that I was completely happy to carry on with my hobbies and casual IT projects over here in London, without any additional help. We are both very comfortably off, and I wish him well in whatever he decides to do. I can categorically guarantee to you that I am no threat to him in any way, either now or at any time in the future, as long as, to quote a famous 'Vulcan' greeting, I live long and prosper."

The two men then lapsed into silence, and looked smilingly at each other while they drank their coffees. Eventually the South African spoke again. "I am sorry to hear you have no interest in joining forces with our mutual acquaintance, as I am sure he will be, but agree you are both equally reliant on the other's continuing goodwill and discretion." With that Botha drained the last of his coffee, stood up and walked purposely out of the cafe, without saying another word or looking back at the ex-Serviceman.

Connolly continued to sit at the table for another ten minutes, while he slowly finished his drink and tried to analyse what had just happened. He was sure that Underwood had no more intention of forming a partnership than he did, so why instigate the meeting? He tried to put himself in Underwood's shoes and think what reason he could have, but try as he might, he could not come up with anything other than Underwood wanted to assess, through Botha, Connelly's potential threat to himself. Then, based on the South African's report, he knew that the solicitor would need to decide what action, if any, he would have to take to safeguard himself, and also what possible consequences those actions might have with regard to his own safety and security. Continuing that line of thought, the ex-Int Corps man thought that if it was him making the decision, he knew that there was only one course of action open to him; remove the threat and deal with the consequences. With that in mind, he stood up and went over to the counter near the door to pay the bill, before returning across the road to his flat, unaware of the two watchers taking up their positions on either side of his building. They were part of a specialist team of four men from Botha's company, who had also tailed Connolly earlier to the solicitors. They had been following him now for five days, as one part of the South African's plan to try and discover as much as possible about Brian Connolly, including assessing how much of a threat he might be to both his employer, Jonathon T Underwood, and himself.

On returning to his flat, Connolly booted up his laptop, opened his email account and went to the message he had received earlier from his ex-Int Corps colleague, regarding potential Service contacts over in Belfast. He wrote down all the names and their details in his notebook, took out a new, unused PAYG phone, and called the first number on the list.

Chapter 26

After a short pause the South African replied, "Good afternoon Jonathon, I hope you had an enjoyable trip back to the UK?"

"I did indeed, although obviously it would have been greatly improved if Abigail had agreed to see me while I was there. What do you have for me?" the solicitor asked, returning to what he knew was Andre's reason for calling him.

"As you asked, we have carried out extensive research into Brian Connolly's history, or as much as we could find in the time available, and also his current activities. I have also met up with the gentleman myself as you requested, and the conclusions I have made from our investigations, I think confirms the opinions I had already started to form about his character, and the potential consequences of your wish to exact revenge upon him for his part in your present circumstances." The South African paused, waiting for any initial reaction from Underwood, and when he remained silent, Andre continued.

"Firstly, our meeting and my conclusions from it. Connolly struck me as being a very confident, strong-minded individual, who was not in the least bit intimidated by me or my organisation, both of which I am sure he has fully researched, or the potential danger he must know he is in from you, after the death of his ex-partner Chief Superintendent Radcliffe. That, to me, confirms our suspicions, that he has made the necessary arrangements to publish all the incriminating evidence he must hold regarding both our criminal histories, in the event of his unexpected and sudden death." Again, Andre paused, and then continued once more after Underwood remained silent.

"Following on from that, in order to safely execute your intentions towards Connolly without us both ending up in prison, we would need to find a way to stop the publication of the said incriminating evidence. That would obviously involve first discovering where it was, if indeed there is only one copy of it, which by the way I seriously doubt. Having found where and how the evidence is being stored, we would then have to either destroy it or find a way to stop its publication. Which brings me on to Connolly's present-day activities. I deployed a four-man surveillance team to follow his every movement over the last few weeks, and he splits his time, apart from the occasional trip out to eat and drink at local restaurants and pubs, between going to a Veteran's Community Group in Lewisham, where he holds IT courses for ex-Service personnel, and working from his flat, where he dabbles in the stocks and money markets. Perhaps dabbles is not really the most appropriate term to use, as according to gossip, one of my own ex-Servicemen employees, who has recently spent some time at the centre, picked up. It is in fact something he has been very successful at, no doubt using the rather large fortune he had already amassed during his criminal activities, to fund his ventures. During his visits to the Vets' Centre, he is mixing with many ex-Service personnel, including men who have their own investigation and security businesses, or connections to them, any one of which he could have deposited the incriminating evidence with for safe keeping. In fact, my man discovered that Connolly help set up one such successful investigation business a couple of years ago; perhaps that is also who helped him discover your present identity and whereabouts. Also, it might be just coincidence, although I don't personally believe in such things, the morning before I met up with him, Connolly paid a visit to his solicitor's office. All this tells me that he could have deposited whatever information he has with a number of different people; the solicitor, his ex-Army colleagues, either singularly or in more than one location, and there is no way we will be able to even identify them, let alone stop its publication. My very strong recommendation to you Jonathon, is that you forget about Mr Connolly, at least for the time being, and wait to see if some other opportunity arises sometime in the future, which presents the possibility of a far less risky outcome for us both."

There was silence for a short while as Jonathon digested Andre's report. He quietly accepted that what the South African said made perfect sense, but that did not make it any more palatable to him. He wanted revenge. Connolly, and his ex-partner Radcliffe, had not only ruined an extremely lucrative, and to him very enjoyable and fulfilling criminal career, but he had also been sentenced to permanent exile, and lost his beloved wife because of their actions. Finally, the solicitor spoke.

"I understand your conclusions Andre and, although it doesn't sit well with me, I am prepared to go along with them for the foreseeable future," the solicitor agreed, knowing that without Andre's help, it would undoubtedly prove very difficult for him to carry out any potential retribution against the ex-Int Corps serviceman. "Please continue to keep me informed of any changes that might arise concerning Connolly's circumstances, and hopefully it's something we can revisit before too long."

The South African breathed a sigh of relief, having been unsure how Underwood would take his report and subsequent recommendations. After a further brief exchange, agreeing to leave any action regarding Connolly for the time being, the two men said their goodbyes and concluded the call.

Underwood sat for a while longer in silence, considering everything that the South African had said. Despite what he had promised to Andre, Underwood knew that he would not be able to let the situation continue as it was. Whatever the consequences, Jonathon resolved to at least attempt to exact his revenge on Connolly, even if it led to his own imprisonment, or worse, if Andre also ended up being incriminated through their past associations.

Chapter 27

Connolly had spotted the first member of the surveillance team following him, the day after his meeting with the South African, Andre Botha. He suspected that he might be being watched, and it was only because he was looking for possible 'tails' that he saw him, as he made his way to the Vets' Centre in Lewisham to hold another of his IT courses for former Servicemen. After that, he soon identified the other three who made up the usual four-man team. He was quite happy to have them for company, because it meant that Underwood and Botha were still assessing the situation, and had obviously not come to a decision as to their future plans concerning himself. While this status quo remained, he would have time to put into action the plan he had formulated over the last couple of days. In his own mind, he was convinced that he had to take action or, sooner or later, he knew they would come for him.

As usual, he had committed his plan to paper, sitting at the coffee table in his flat, writing down his objectives and subsequent courses of action in his small notebook, clarifying everything in his mind, in order to know exactly what he needed to do to stay alive. Everything, he knew, rested on his assumption that Underwood would at some stage initiate some kind of action against himself, so he would need to eliminate that threat before it was set in motion. In other words, remove Underwood before he had chance to do the same to himself. He had two options, the first and most desirable, was to make it look as though he was in no way involved. The second and back-up plan, which would probably also result in his own arrest, was less desirable but at least it might, with a little luck, mean only a prison sentence, and not necessarily his own death.

Objectives

Plan A

1. Offer Underwood possibility of future partnership.
2. Invite him to London for meeting.
3. Inform interested partners of time, date, place of meeting.
4. Disappear while 3 above occurs.
5. If operation successful, delay return to London for a couple of weeks in order to let things settle.
6. Contact AB for reaction.

Plan B

1. If nothing comes of Plan A, inform Scotland Yard of Underwood's location while he is in London.
2. As 4, 5 and 6 above.

Having gone over the plan several times, and concluding it was his best chance of survival, he took out one of his new, unused PAYG phones, and called the solicitor's office in Dubai, hoping that Underwood would be there. His call was answered almost immediately.

"Good afternoon," Underwood said, waiting for the caller to announce who they were.

"Good afternoon Jonathon, it's Brian Connolly. How are you?" the ex-Int Corps serviceman replied. "I thought I would give you a call. After my meeting with your South African associate, I have been doing some thinking, and I may have been a little hasty in dismissing your offer of a possible partnership out of hand. Perhaps, as you suggested, we should meet up for a chat."

The solicitor immediately sat up in his chair, his mind now fully alert, thinking how he could capitalise on this unexpected opportunity. "I am very pleased to hear that Brian. What do you suggest?" he replied, trying not to sound too enthusiastic.

"If we are to meet up Jonathon, I would prefer it to be over here in the UK. I would not, as you previously proposed, be happy coming over to Dubai," Connolly answered. "Are you planning a trip over here in the near future?" he continued.

"As it happens Brian, yes, I will be over next month with my employers for a week or so, finalising some house purchases. I will let you know the dates when I have them. Where do you suggest we meet?" Underwood asked, overjoyed at this unexpected chance to perhaps have the opportunity, so soon, to exact revenge on this man who had helped to ruin his life.

"Somewhere public, probably in London, but where we will both feel safe. I will give it some thought, and let you know a couple of options once we know the dates when you are coming over," Connolly suggested.

"Sounds good Brian. I will look forward to it," Underwood agreed and they concluded the call.

Connolly had not seen his 'followers' for a couple of days, and now that he had proposed meeting the solicitor, he was very confident that Underwood, if he had not already, would remove the surveillance team, and thus allow the ex-Int Corps man the freedom to move around unobserved.

So, having successfully initiated his preferred plan of action, Connolly took out the two folders of information he had already put together, in anticipation of the next steps he had decided to take.

The first contained a white envelope, with a Belfast resident and address typed on it, and a single sheet of paper with the following, also typed, and a copy of one of the photographs taken of Underwood in Dubai.

Jonathon T Jones (aka Underwood, presently residing in Dubai)

Declan & Jimmy McConnell (Liverpool)

Mick & Aileen O'Hare

Jerry Duggan

Smuggled gemstones and drugs

JTJ/U coming to London shortly. Will contact you with more information.

Please email me a secure mobile number for contact at 'anonymous246@londonnet.org'

The second file contained a memory stick, which contained everything that Connolly had put together on Jonathon T Underwood and his past criminal activities, plus all the information regarding the solicitor's new life in Dubai, including the photographs taken of him there. He had purposely removed anything that might incriminate Andre Botha from the file, still hoping to avoid any conflict with the South African or his organisation. This package was addressed to Detective Inspector Richard Greenwood, c/o New Scotland Yard, Victoria Embankment, London SW1A 2JL.

He would post the letter to Belfast, once he had agreed the details of his proposed meeting with Underwood. The jiffy bag containing the memory stick and the information regarding Underwood's life in Dubai to Scotland Yard, as a back up to his main plan in case it did not work out as he hoped, he would post at a later date, probably the week before his meeting with the solicitor. Or perhaps he could leave it with ex-Captain Tony Cunningham for safe keeping along with the more fulsome information he had already given him in case of his unexpected demise, he had not decided as yet. He would then, if required, have his second option of informing DI Greenwood anonymously of Underwood's presence in London, if he felt that was his last resort.

The final part of his plan was to be well away from London when, he hoped, Underwood was finally removed as a threat to himself. To that end, he took out his laptop and once the 'Google' page appeared, he typed in

'Campervan' and tapped the 'return' key. There immediately appeared a list of 'links' to a large number of websites, offering every type and size of mobile home. It took him a while, and several different sites, before he found exactly what he was looking for. It was a site which listed a large number of 'Campervans for private sale', and the vehicle he was searching for, which read:

2019 VW Transporter Trendline 4-Berth Campervan.

46,000 miles, one owner from new, with full service history & 12 months MOT.

1 year RAC Platinum Warranty.

Copper Bronze 2-litre Diesel.

£48k cash sale only.

Collect or will deliver.

Call or email for more information.

No time wasters please.

Connolly immediately called the mobile number on the advert, and was pleased to hear that the campervan was still available. He arranged to meet the vendor the following day, at the address of an industrial unit on the outskirts of South London, to check the vehicle out, and hopefully conclude the sale. He had already planned the route for his temporary disappearance. Once he bought the campervan, he would drive it down to Heathrow Airport and park it in the 'Long Stay' carpark, before taking the train back to London. When he was ready to 'disappear', he would return to Heathrow by train with his luggage, like any other potential holiday maker. He would then take the airport bus back out to the long stay carpark and pick up his campervan, before driving in his newly acquired mobile home around the M25 and joining the A1, for the drive up to his house in Newcastle, where he would pick up his camping and hiking gear. He would then continue up the A1 into Scotland, and then eventually onto The Highlands of Northern Scotland by a circuitous route, where he would disappear from sight, until he deemed it safe for him to return to London, hopefully with Underwood removed from the picture, either permanently or arrested. Either way, on his return, he would then have to deal with Andre Botha, something he was not particularly looking forward to. Having now made his plans, he relaxed, sure in the knowledge that he had now given himself the best possible chance of at least getting out of the situation he now found himself in with his life, and hopefully if everything went to plan, his continued freedom.

Chapter 28

The day following his unexpected call from Brian Connolly, Underwood confirmed with the Sheik's personal assistant the dates of their forthcoming trip back to the UK, to complete the house purchases and the furnishing of the two properties. Having made a note of the times of the flights out and back in his online diary, he then sent two texts from two different PAYG phones. The first to a PAYG phone in Liverpool and the second to a similar phone in London.

The text to Declan McConnell in Liverpool simply read "Coming over shortly, will need your help. Call ASAP."

The second text was to Brian Connolly, confirming the dates he would be over in London, and asking where and when he would like to meet.

The PAYG phone he had used to text Declan rang almost immediately.

"Morning Declan," the solicitor answered. "Thank you for calling back so promptly."

"No problem," the joint Managing Director of McConnell's Transport & Warehousing Limited, one of Underwood's 'silent' partners and longstanding friends, "I presumed it must be important. What can I do for you?"

"I am coming over to London at the beginning of next month for a couple of weeks, and I am going to need you and your brother to assist me with a potentially serious problem I have," Underwood said. "With the help of Andre, I have finally identified the mystery IT man who was Radcliffe's partner, and who orchestrated the theft of our money."

"Have you indeed Jonathon, that's great news. Does he know that you know?" Declan asked.

"Yes, in fact we have been in dialogue recently, and I have been spinning him a story that I want to go into partnership with him, in order to gain his trust. Unfortunately he has discovered my new identity and life over here, and he has intimated that he could share that information with the police if I don't agree to his terms. In short Declan he now poses a threat to all our liberties, so I have decided to remove that particular threat permanently," Underwood lied, in order to get the two brothers to help him with Connolly's execution. The solicitor knew he could not go to his South African henchman, and since the McConnell brothers were unaware of Connolly's memory stick 'insurance package', and the subsequent risk to all of them through their potential exposure to the police if anything fatal was to happen to the ex-Int Corps serviceman, Underwood was happy to use the twin brothers' ignorance of their own potential danger, to further his own ends. If that meant them all going to prison following Brian Connelly's death, so be it he reasoned.

"Why aren't you using Botha?" Declan asked, knowing that Jonathon had used the South African's services in Northern Ireland, and no doubt on other occasions, for such dangerous assignments.

"Andre pointed out that it would be too risky for his organisation," the solicitor lied. "As several of his operatives who do that kind of work are ex-Servicemen themselves, and as Connelly is heavily involved with the Vets' Community Centre in London, he thought, and I agreed, that there was a chance that Connolly might be tipped off about the operation from one of his own contacts," Underwood continued with his fabrication.

"Okay, what do you want us to do Jonathon?" Declan asked.

"As I said, I have suggested to Connolly that we join forces, and so are going to meet up at some stage during my trip to discuss these imaginary plans. Once I have the time, actual date and place of our meeting, we will need to engineer a way to dispose of our Mr Connolly. Our meeting will be in a public place, so it will need to happen either before we actually meet up, or shortly afterwards, and certainly before I return to Dubai. I will contact you again Declan once I have the meeting details, then we can arrange to get together at my hotel beforehand and discuss how, where and when we will carry it out."

"Sounds good Jonathon, we will be ready," Declan confirmed and Jonathon ended the call.

As he was speaking to his friend and colleague in Liverpool, the other PAYG phone on his desk 'pinged', announcing an incoming text. It was from Brian Connolly, thanking him for the details of his forthcoming trip to London, and suggesting that perhaps they could meet up at the solicitor's hotel in the public bar, on the Wednesday or Thursday of the second week of his trip, around 11am.

Connolly said that he was holding an IT course at the Vets' centre during the first week of Underwood's visit, so it would be more convenient then, and that the suggestion of Underwood's hotel's public bar was for his own and the solicitor's peace of mind. The real reason, although as it happened he was holding an IT course at the Vet's Centre that week, was that it would give him time to formulate his own plans regarding Underwood before disappearing himself. He had no intention of being in London after that first week, and he needed to know which hotel Underwood would be staying at, in order to pass that information on to Belfast.

Underwood happily texted back his agreement to Connolly's suggestions, confirming his hotel details and suggesting that they meet on the Thursday at 12am in the Grosvenor Bar on the ground floor, directly behind his hotel's reception area.

On receiving the confirmation text and Underwood's hotel details and the dates of his visit, Connolly replied with a 'thumbs up' emoji, before copying all this information onto the letter to Belfast, which he would post later that afternoon.

All that now remained for Connolly to do, to complete his initial preparations, was to pick up his newly acquired campervan from South London, and drive it down to Heathrow Airport's 'Long Stay' carpark, before returning to London to await, hopefully, for a response to his Belfast letter. If he received nothing back from them over the next week or so, then he would regretfully have to resort to his back-up plan, which involved informing the police of Underwood's new persona and life in Dubai, or even perhaps of his imminent trip to London. Either of these two alternative scenarios would undoubtedly prove very dangerous to himself, and would almost certainly end up in his own arrest, or worse if Andre Botha also became drawn into everything, something he was desperately trying to avoid. It was a desperate plan he knew, but at least it held out the possibility of success.

Chapter 29

Connolly, with an enormous sigh of relief, received an email reply to the letter he sent to Belfast a week after posting it, and two weeks before Jonathon Underwood's forthcoming trip to London. It was more in hope than expectation that he had sent the letter, in his heart of hearts believing nothing would come of it, and he would then have to go down the route of informing on the exiled solicitor, a course of action which would inevitably lead to his own arrest, or possibly worse if the South African became involved.

The email simply confirmed the receipt of the letter and the information contained therein, the recipient's interest and a mobile number on which he could be contacted.

Connolly immediately sent a text to the mobile, acknowledging his receipt of their email and promising that he would be in touch shortly, with a further update regarding Underwood's presence in London.

The ex-Int Corps man then rang his friend Tony Cunningham on his personal mobile phone, the man who had helped him, through his private investigation company, discover Underwood's new identity and life in Dubai.

His call was answered eventually after several rings, and the ex-Captain came on the line.

"Morning Brian, how are you?" he answered, and continued before Connolly could reply. "What can I do for you? I am a bit tied up at the moment, sorry, but can you keep it brief old chap," Cunningham asked, sounding a little flustered.

"Yes, sorry to bother you Tony," Connolly said quickly. "I will need your help in a couple of weeks' time, with some surveillance work here in London, plus I have another package for you which I would like you to keep for me. I will drop it off for you at the Vet's Centre with the Major if that is alright with you."

"Okay, no problem. Give me a call back later today with the details, say around 4pm," and with that Cunningham immediately ended the call.

Connolly put a reminder on his phone diary to call Tony back at 4pm, and then made a call to the number on the campervan advertisement, hoping to be able to go down and complete its purchase, as agreed, later that afternoon. Fortunately, he was informed that the van would be available for collection, so after checking the times of the trains from Victoria Station, to take him down to where it was being garaged South of London, he set off to the Underground with a large sports bag, containing the cash in neat bundles of £50 notes.

The journey and purchase of his new campervan went off without a hitch, and he was soon on his way to Heathrow Airport, where he drove into the main Long Stay carpark and parked his new purchase, before boarding an airport bus to take him back to the main terminal building. He then walked to the airport train terminal, before boarding the Heathrow Express train back to Paddington Station and then the Underground, arriving back at his flat just after 3:30pm.

After a quick shower and change of clothes, he made himself a large mug of tea, before calling Tony Cunningham back at precisely 4pm.

Cunningham answered the call on the second ring. "Afternoon Brian, thanks for calling back and sorry about this morning," the head of Guards Security & Investigations Ltd. apologised, sounding a lot more relaxed than he had in the morning. "I was in the middle of a bit of a situation, but it is all sorted out now thankfully."

"No problem Tony, fully understand," Connolly replied.

"So, what is it you would like me to do for you?" ex-Captain Cunningham asked.

"It's to do with that investigation you did for me a few weeks ago. The chap you identified for me who lives in Dubai, Jonathon Jones, is coming over to London for a visit, and I would like you to keep an eye on him for me if you could, nothing more than that. I will text you the dates of his trip and where he is staying. I would like to know his room number at the hotel as soon as possible after he arrives, and where he goes and who he meets. I still don't trust him, if you know what I mean, and I would like to know what he is up to over here. It goes without saying, that it is of paramount importance that he does not suspect you are watching or following him, so please don't take any undue risks. I will be running one of my IT courses at the Vets' Centre during the first week of his visit, so you can update me there or by phone if you like. I will also drop that package off at the Centre for your safe keeping, if you don't have time to pop in yourself and pick it up. It is a sealed A4 brown envelope with my initials printed on the front. Inside there is another package which contains some sensitive information, which I may or may not need you to post for me if I am away on my next job. Sorry it is all a bit cloak and dagger but I will explain everything to you eventually I promise. Again I can assure you that there is nothing illegal or criminal in what I am asking you to do, both packages are forms of insurance which I will only use if I have to." Connolly paused, to allow the ex-Captain to comment or ask him something regarding his instructions, but when the line remained silent, he continued. "After the course, on the following Monday, I will be off for a couple of weeks on a job, so if you could let me know anything you find out before then, I would be very grateful."

"Fully understand Brian, and will be happy to oblige," Cunningham confirmed, wondering to himself what his friend and ex-army colleague was taking all these precautions for. However he knew better than to question the ex-Int Corps man, and after saying their goodbyes the two ex-army colleagues ended the call.

Connolly then sat down with his mug of tea on his favourite armchair, and went over the strategy he had formulated again in his head. He was sure he had done all he could to facilitate the success of the plan; everything now depended on how the people in Belfast reacted to the information he had supplied to them and whether, as he hoped, they would seek retribution for Underwood's actions against some of their own, and reply in kind to the executions of their fellow Irishmen and woman.

It was the day after Underwood's planned arrival in the UK that Connolly received his first message from ex-Captain Tony Cunningham, and it simply read, "Jones is staying in room 247. TC".

Connolly immediately texted back, "Excellent Tony. Many thanks. BC".

He then texted that same information to the number that had been emailed to him from Belfast, unaware that the phone that received the message was already sitting on a bedside cabinet in room 301, in the same hotel that Underwood/Jones was staying in.

Chapter 30

Underwood returned to his hotel in the late afternoon on the second day of his London trip, after a visit to the solicitor handling the sale of the first of the two houses, that his employer had decided to purchase in Newmarket. The owner of the large, five-bedroom house seemed to be having second thoughts on selling the property, either that or he was trying to get a higher price, now that he knew who the purchaser was. It had been a fraught day of negotiations at the Newmarket solicitor's office, and on entering his room, Underwood, after dropping his briefcase and suit jacket onto the large leather Chesterfield sofa in his executive suite, went straight to the 'minibar' and took out a couple of the small bottles of premium lager, and poured the contents into one of the large glasses which he retrieved from the tray on an adjoining side table. He took the drink and sat down on the matching Chesterfield armchair, slowly unwinding from the trials and tribulations of the day. After finally draining the last of the lager, he retrieved one of the PAYG phones he had brought with him from his bedside cabinet, and called the only number in the phone's directly, which was answered almost immediately.

"Afternoon Jonathon," came the quick reply, "we were wondering when you would call."

"Afternoon yourself Declan. I trust you are both well?" Jonathon asked cheerily, before continuing. "Where are you, nearby I hope?"

"We are fine thanks, and yes, we managed to get a hotel about half a mile from you."

"Excellent; can you both come over to my hotel this evening, say about 8pm? We could meet in the Grosvenor Bar behind reception," Underwood suggested.

"Okay Jonathon, we'll see you then," Declan confirmed, and then the two men ended the call.

At just before 8pm, after enjoying a very pleasant meal in the hotel's main residents' restaurant, Jonathon entered the Grosvenor Bar, which although it was still early in the evening, only had a couple of vacant tables and all the booths were taken. Fortunately, as Jonathon walked into the bar looking around for somewhere to sit, he spotted that the McConnell twin brothers were already there, and had in fact managed to get the last free four-seater booth at the back of the bar. Smiling, Jonathon walked over to them, and sat down next to the brothers on the semi-circular bench seat.

"How long have you been here?" Jonathon asked, looking at both of them and their half empty pint glasses, of what looked like lager.

"Probably about twenty-five minutes," Declan replied. "It was Jimmy's idea to come early just to have a look around, and it's a good job we did. This was the last free booth when we arrived, otherwise we could have ended up in the middle of everyone else."

"Well done Jimmy, good move," the solicitor acknowledged. "It's the first time I have been in here and did not realise how popular it was. I'll just go and get myself a drink and then you can tell me what you have been up to." With that, Jonathon walked over to the bar and returned shortly afterwards with a large glass of red wine.

"I have just eaten a rather large, extremely pleasant meal," Jonathon said in explanation to the quizzical looks of the two brothers at his choice of drink, as he sat back down, placing the glass of wine on the table beside their two pints.

Once they had each taken a drink from their respective glasses, Declan, being the main spokesman for the twins, opened the conversation. "We arrived yesterday and spent today getting our bearings, especially having a good look at Connolly's apartment building and the surrounding area, and we also had a walk through that Veteran's place in Lewisham you told us about. Connolly was there, as you said he would be, holding the IT course in one of the main Community Centre Rooms next door."

What they did not know, and had not spotted, was that there were two other men who were keeping Connolly's apartment under surveillance. They had seen the two brothers approach the building, arousing the watchers' suspicions as the twins obviously appeared to be looking at Connolly's apartment block and the surrounding area. The watchers then 'tailed' the brothers to the Vets' Centre, again where they had a good look around, before following them both back to their hotel. Those same two men, having received instructions from their superior, had now attached themselves to the brothers, along with another two-man team from the same company, and all four were now sat at two separate tables in the Grosvenor Bar, covertly monitoring the meeting between Underwood and the twins. Also sat at the bar, on one of the high stools, was ex-Captain Anthony Cunningham, who was also very interested in the exiled solicitor and his two new guests.

"And what do you think?" Underwood asked.

"We think the apartment is really the only option," Declan replied immediately. "We will have to get in somehow, either by you talking your way in and us following, or forcing an entry while he is out and waiting for his return."

"Yes, that's what I had concluded, and neither way is particularly appealing," Jonathon agreed. "The apartment has a very sophisticated alarm system consisting of pressure sensors and video camera surveillance all linked, I think, to Connolly's laptop and smart phone. Our chances of taking him by surprise are somewhere between extremely slim and non-existent. I am due to see him in here a week on Thursday, after the course he is running this week has concluded, so we have plenty of time to look at alternative strategies before then. I think we should wait until after I have met up with him before we decide how to proceed, if only to see what he has to say. Also, hopefully by then, I will have concluded my business here for the Sheik, so that will also give me some time with you to formulate our best possible options. You two continue to keep Connolly under surveillance in the meantime, and keep me informed of anything you find out that might help us. It's probably best if we don't meet up again until next week."

"Okay Jonathon," Declan agreed, before quickly finishing his drink, and signalling to his brother to do the same. They both then stood up and left the bar and returned to their hotel, leaving Jonathon to finish his glass of wine, before returning himself, fifteen minutes later, to his own room.

What none of the three conspirators noticed, was that the two new members of the four-man surveillance team also rose from their table on the other side of the bar as the McConnell brothers left, and followed them out, leaving the other two-man team, who had originally been outside Connolly's apartment, watching Jonathon.

Also present in the Grosvenor Bar, observing the meeting between the McConnell brothers and Jonathon Underwood, and unaware of the four other 'watchers' who were monitoring the meeting along with ex-Captain Cunningham, were the occupants of room 301, registered as a Mr & Mrs Sean Farrell from Belfast, but whose real names were Mr & Mrs Kieran O'Hare. Kieran was the head of one of Belfast's most notorious non-paramilitary crime families, brother to the previously murdered Mick and Aileen O'Hare, and the name on the letter Brian Connolly had posted to Belfast a couple of weeks earlier. Kieran could not believe his luck when he had recognised the McConnell twins, the other two names listed in the anonymous letter he had received and implicated, along with Jones (aka Underwood), in his brother's and sister-in-law's executions.

Shortly after the McConnell brothers had returned to their hotel, one of their two 'tails' made a call to his company's Managing Director, with a full report of the evening's events.

At the same time as that report was being received, Kieran O'Hare was calling back to Belfast from his hotel room, ordering another two of his colleagues to travel over to London on the next available flight, and ex-Captain Cunningham was speaking to Brian Connolly, also giving him a full report of the meeting between the man who he knew as Jonathon Jones, and what appeared to be two brothers, who were so alike that he thought they might be twins.

Chapter 31

Brian Connolly was taken by surprise with the report that Tony Cunningham delivered to him, following the ex-Captain's evening watching Jonathon in the Grosvenor Bar, and the solicitor's meeting with the two newcomers on the scene. Connolly knew instantly that the mysterious men were Underwood's associates from Liverpool, the brothers Declan and Jimmy McConnell. What concerned him was the fact that they were here in London; surely, it could not just be coincidence he thought. Connolly knew he had been, and probably still was being, observed covertly by the South African's team, so why would Underwood need them here as well? The only conclusion he could come to, was that the McConnells were working independently for Underwood, without Botha's knowledge, and that pointed to the solicitor looking to take some direct action himself, and probably quite soon. Connolly immediately decided he could not wait until after the IT course he was running, before putting the final parts of his plan into action.

At 9:30am the following morning, he called Major Whyatt at the Vets' Centre, asking him to pass on his sincere apologies to the six veterans who were attending the introductory computing and internet course, but he would have to postpone the last two days of their course, as he had been called away on another very urgent matter. He also asked him to pass on the package he had left with him for Tony Cunningham the previous day. The

Major was less than impressed, and after unsuccessfully trying to get a more detailed reason why Connolly was being called away, finally agreed to pass on his message to, the no doubt, very disappointed Veterans, and the package to Cunningham when he next came into the Centre.

Connolly then called Tony Cunningham, telling him that he had unexpectantly been called away on a very urgent contract, reminded him to pick up the package he had left for him with the Major, and that he would not be contactable for a while. However, he asked Cunningham to continue his surveillance of 'Mr Jones', and to update him on anything of interest, and he gave him an email address which he could be reached on. When Tony finally queried him about the two packages, Connolly vaguely explained that, as he had said before, they were just something he might have to use in an emergency, but that in the meantime he asked his friend to keep them safe and that he would let him know what to do with either of them, if required. Connelly sensed that his friend was beginning to feel uneasy about holding the two different packages, what they might contain, and what were the particular circumstances that Connelly was vaguely referring to, when he would have to use one, or both of them. However, Connolly knew he could not take the ex-Captain into his confidence, without implicating him in what could turn into a very serious situation, both with Underwood and Botha, and the forces of law and order, if things did not turn out as he hoped.

Cunningham finally accepted that the ex-Int Corps man was not going to enlighten him any further, which actually was no big surprise to him, and he agreed to do as he was requested, before the two men ended the call.

Shortly after his call to Tony, the ex-Int Corps man ordered a taxi from a local firm, to arrive in two hours' time to take him to Paddington Station, giving himself plenty of time to pack.

Ten minutes before the pre-arranged time, Connolly was stood outside his apartment building entrance, with a large suitcase and the specially designed backpack, which contained his laptop and its ancillary equipment, in plain view of the two 'watchers' sitting in 'Ron's Place' across the road. When the taxi pulled up beside him, Connolly saw the two men exit the café and start walking across the road in his general direction, chatting to each other as they occasionally casually glanced towards him. Connolly, unnecessarily as the driver already knew his fare's destination, loudly confirmed to the private hire driver, as he got out of his vehicle to load the baggage into his boot, that he was "Connolly for Paddington Station please". As soon as Connolly had got into the taxi and it had set off, one of the two 'watchers' took out his mobile and immediately made a call to their two colleagues, who were sat in a silver BMW 3 series saloon just round the corner from the apartment building. "He has just got into a black Audi estate car from ABC Taxis, and is on his way to Paddington Station with a suitcase and backpack."

"Roger that," came the reply, and the BMW set off in pursuit of the black taxi.

As the taxi had started its journey from close by, the BMW soon picked it up, knowing which route it would probably take, and had no difficulty staying a couple of cars behind it all the way to Paddington, where they saw Connolly get out at the main drop-off point and then carry his luggage into the station. One of the two 'tails' also got out at the same drop-off area shortly after Connolly, while the driver of the BMW drove round to the short stay carpark nearby, to wait for his colleague.

He did not have long to wait, no more than fifteen minutes, when his partner returned from following Connolly.

"He got on the Heathrow Express. What do we do now?" he asked.

"Better phone base and see what they want us to do," his partner replied, taking out his phone.

Once they had spoken to their supervisor, who in turn had referred to his boss, and having been finally told to return to the office, they turned the car round and headed back to the city centre.

Connolly had spotted the 'watchers' coming out of 'Ron's Place', and the silver BMW tailing them to Paddington, which was fine by him. He knew there was no way they could get to Heathrow in time to see him take the airport bus back to the Long Stay carpark and pick up his campervan, which he duly did and set off unnoticed on his planned escape from London.

By the time, much later that day when Kieran O'Hare, who was sitting in his hotel room with his two colleagues, would be trying to locate the McConnell brothers, and Underwood would receive his unexpected visit from

LOOSE ENDS

Andre Botha, the ex-Int Corps man was already at his house just up the road from St James's Park in Newcastle, loading up the campervan with everything he would need for his extended trip around the highlands of Scotland. Connolly intended to set off early the following morning, and be well away from any possible discovery by the various potentially interested parties back in London, or at least until he decided it was safe to return, with hopefully Underwood ceasing to be a threat to him.

Chapter 32

Jonathon returned to his hotel after a far more successful, and problem-free, day at the offices of the solicitor who was handling the sale of the second, and the far more imposing and luxurious property of the two that his employer had decided to purchase. The present owner had already vacated, what, in essence, was a small 'estate', and moved abroad, so was keen to complete the sale as soon as possible, especially as he had already inflated the asking price of the property quite considerably from its actual market value.

He quickly undressed, having decided to have a shower before going down to the hotel's restaurant, and sampling some more of their excellent cuisine. Just before he was about to enter the shower, his room phone started to ring, but deciding it probably was nothing important, he ignored it and continued into the bathroom.

Ten minutes later, when he re-emerged from his refreshing shower, Jonathon noticed that there was a small, red flashing light on the bedroom phone indicating, he presumed, a message had been left for him. He quickly dried himself and dressed again in clean, casual clothes before picking up the handset and pressing the flashing button. The system informed him that he had one message and to press '1' to play it, which he duly did. A female voice asked him to please call reception on '100'. Jonathon quickly dialled the number and was immediately connected.

"Good evening, Reception, how may I help you?" came the prompt reply.

"Yes, good evening. I have a message on my phone to call you; it's Jonathon Jones in Room 247," the solicitor answered, fortunately remembering to use his 'new' public persona, and the name he was registered under at the hotel.

"Just hold a moment please, sir." There was a short pause and then the receptionist spoke again. "There is a gentleman asking to see you sir. He came in about fifteen minutes ago and is waiting in the main foyer for you; he said his name is Andre Botha. He said he was happy to wait."

Andre's presence at the hotel shocked Jonathon, as he had purposely not informed the South African of his visit to the UK. He had hoped to carry out his plans, before Botha could prevent him from taking his revenge on Connolly, actions which undoubtedly would put them both in jeopardy. So, the first question was, how did Andre know he was here, and secondly, and probably more importantly, why was he taking such a risk meeting him here in public? After a pause, while these thoughts quickly ran through his mind, Jonathon finally spoke again to the young lady on reception. "Please apologise to Mr Botha for the delay, as I was just taking a shower. Tell him I will be down in a couple of minutes." With that, Jonathon replaced the receiver and, knowing that now he was probably going to have to delay his plans concerning Connolly at least for the immediate future, he left his room and walked down the couple of flights of stairs leading to the hotel reception. On entering the reception foyer, Jonathon soon spotted Andre sitting in one of the large armchairs and walked over to him, extending his right hand as he approached the smiling South African, who quickly stood up and firmly shook the solicitor's hand.

"Good evening Andre," Jonathon greeted him quietly. "What a pleasant surprise. Should we go through to the Grosvenor," he continued, and without waiting for a reply, led Andre through to the bar and to one of the empty booths at the rear of the room. Jonathon indicated to his guest to sit down before speaking again.

"What would you like to drink," Jonathon asked.

"I'll have a glass of fresh orange with some ice, if I may," answered the South African, with a smile.

"Won't be a minute," Jonathon replied as he turned and went over to the bar, before returning shortly afterwards with two glasses of fresh orange and ice, which he put down on the table, before sitting down opposite Andre.

After a short silence, while the two men each took a drink of their orange juice, the South African finally spoke.

"I am surprised you did not let me know you were coming over to London, Jonathon," Andre said, still smiling. "In fact, I am a little disappointed," he added, a slight edge creeping into his voice.

After another short silence Jonathon replied, still wondering how Botha first of all knew he was here in London, and secondly his reason for this unannounced meeting, although he was already forming an idea what it might be. "It is just a short business trip Andre, tying up the legal paperwork for the purchase of a couple of residences for the Sheik. I did not think it was worth notifying you, as I do not require any of your services," he answered, knowing that even if that were true, he should still have let his friend know of his impending visit out of courtesy at least, and also for his own security while he was in the UK.

"And your meeting with the McConnell brothers, was that to do with your business for the Sheik or something else?" the South African asked, more menacingly now, but still continuing to smile across at an obviously stunned Underwood, who just sat quietly, not knowing how to reply, having been taken completely off guard by Andre's question.

Botha also sat in silence for a short while before again continuing. "I feared you might not take my advice regarding Connolly, even though the consequences of your possible actions, for both of us, could undoubtedly be very serious. You might not care Jonathon about serving a lengthy sentence in prison, but I certainly do. So, I have been keeping a watchful eye on our IT man, purely as a precaution for my own safety, and when one of my teams spotted your Liverpudlian associates having a look around Connolly's apartment and the Veteran's Centre, followed by your meeting with them here at the hotel, I feared the worst." Again, the South African paused to allow Underwood to speak. When the solicitor declined and continued to sit in silence, Andre drunk the last of his orange before standing up and speaking again. "Jonathon,

I expect you to abandon whatever plans you have made, or were about to make, with the McConnells, complete your business with the Sheik, and return home to Dubai. I will continue to keep an eye both on Connelly, and you and the McConnells, until you are safely back home. Again, I must insist that you leave Connelly alone until an opportunity arises, perhaps sometime in the future, when we can deal with the situation safely, and without the possibility of either of us going to prison."

With that, Andre left a completely deflated Underwood to finish his drink, before the solicitor slowly wandered through to the restaurant, for what turned out to be a far less enjoyable meal than he had initially anticipated.

As Underwood and the South African were having their meeting in the Grosvenor Bar, Kieran O'Hare was sitting in his room, along with his wife, briefing his two trusted, fellow gang members, Ardal and Fergal, regarding the reason for their unexpected summons to London. Ardal and Fergal were the two main 'enforcers' in Kieran's criminal organisation, and they had flown into Heathrow less than a couple of hours before, and had then travelled directly to Kieran's hotel. After a brief discussion, they formulated a simple plan, and were now on their mobile phones, methodically calling each hotel within the London area, asking to speak to one of their guests called Declan McConnell. It was Ardal who was eventually successful in his request, but before the hotel receptionist could transfer him to McConnell's room, Ardal disconnected the call. The three men then had a further quick discussion, before Fergal called the same hotel back and was fortunate to be able to book a twin room for himself and

Ardal for the next three nights, under false names, and like Kieran, paid for their room in advance with a stolen credit card. After arranging to meet the following evening in their hotel, which would give them time to acquaint themselves with the layout of the place and discover which room, or rooms, the McConnells were occupying, the two newcomers picked up their overnight cases and went back down to the hotel's lobby, before going outside and getting into one of the black cabs which were lined up outside the prestigious hotel.

Chapter 33

Underwood had further appointments at both the properties' solicitors in Newmarket on the Thursday of the first week of his trip to London, the day after his surprise meeting with Andre Botha in his hotel's bar. One was at 11am in the morning and the second at 2:30pm in the afternoon. Both went well, and when he returned to his hotel at just after 6pm with all the necessary paperwork completed for both properties, his mood had improved markedly from the massive disappointment of the previous evening, and Andre's order to him to leave Brian Connelly alone, a directive he knew it would be very wise to follow, however much it frustrated him.

Before taking his usual early evening shower, prior to going down to the hotel's excellent restaurant, he took out the PAYG phone and called Declan McConnell. The call was eventually answered after several rings by a breathless Declan.

"Evening Jonathon, sorry it took so long to answer, but we were just going out of the door to get something to eat in town. We weren't expecting you to call," he said, after rushing back into their room where he had left the phone, to take the call.

"No problem; unfortunately, there is a major change of plan Declan. Having consulted with Andre Botha," the solicitor lied, trying to keep face by making it appear that it was a joint decision and not one that the South African had forced on him, "we have decided to put our plans on hold for the moment. Andre thinks it might be too dangerous to do anything now while we are all together in London, and he has suggested that he should monitor Connolly's movements for a while longer, and hope a better opportunity might arise, away from the city and Connolly's many contacts among the service veterans. I have reluctantly agreed, so you can return home whenever you want. Thank you for coming, and I am very sorry for any inconvenience I may have caused you both. I will of course reimburse you both for all your expenses, plus a little bonus for your trouble."

"Okay Jonathon, whatever you say," a surprised Declan replied, before continuing. "Now that you are over here, we might as well take advantage of it and meet up for a bite to eat somewhere, what do you say? It would be good to have a catch-up before we go back to Liverpool, and you return to Dubai. Who knows when we might have the opportunity again," Declan suggested.

"Yes, excellent idea Declan, how about we do tomorrow evening, about 7:30pm? I will book somewhere close by for all of us, and then we could meet up; I would like that," Jonathon replied.

"Sounds like a plan Jonathon, see you tomorrow evening then," Declan confirmed and the two ended the call.

Jonathon then undressed, and had a very invigorating and refreshing shower, before dressing again in his casual clothes, and going down to the restaurant for his evening meal. He decided to skip the Grosvenor Bar, having had a long and tiring day, and instead opted for an early night and so returned to his room.

He walked back into his room and went over to the minibar, before taking out a miniature bottle of Glenfiddich whiskey, retrieving one of the cut-glass goblets from the tray on the side table, and sitting down with them both on the leather armchair. As he was about to pour the whiskey into the glass, he was startled by the sight of a tall, slim, dark-haired man appearing through his half-open bathroom door, holding a large handgun with a silencer attachment, which was pointed squarely at the centre of his chest.

"Good evening Mr Jones - or should I call you Underwood?" the intruder asked in a strong Belfast accent. "Please don't get up," he said pleasantly, using the gun to signal for Jonathon to sit back down, as the solicitor started to rise up from his chair. "I have been looking forward to meeting you for a long time," he continued, before slowly sitting down himself on the side of the leather sofa farthest from the stunned Underwood, the gun unwaveringly pointing at the solicitor.

After a short silence, Underwood's unexpected guest finally spoke again. "Do you know who I am Jonathon?" he asked quietly, but with a menacing undertone. When Underwood merely shook his head slowly in answer, too shocked and frightened to speak, seeing the calm assurance of the man sat across from him, the intruder continued. "My name is Kieran O'Hare. I believe you had dealings with my brother Mick, his wife Aileen, and a colleague of theirs, Jerry Duggan, some time ago. A dispute over some stolen precious gemstones I believe." Again, the Irishman paused, allowing the solicitor to speak if he so wished, but again Underwood just continued to sit in terrified silence, as the enormity of his perilous predicament was beginning to dawn on him, now that he knew the identity of the man sat across from him holding the silenced handgun, which continued to point steadily at his chest.

"From your continued silence I take it that you have nothing to say?" Kieran asked. In fact Underwood had a lot to say, including the two most important questions - 'How did you find out about me and where I was?', and 'How did you get into my room?', but his brain refused to connect with his vocal chords, and he could only sit in terrified silence looking at the gun that was pointing unerringly at him. The Irishman continued to look at the solicitor quietly for another few seconds, then just as the name 'Connolly' shrieked into Underwood's mind, Kieran calmly shot him twice in the chest. He then stood up again, and walked over to the now inert body of the solicitor, which was slumped in the armchair. Kieran rolled it onto the floor, arranging the body neatly on its back, with the legs together and arms by its sides, before shooting the already dead Underwood once through the centre of his forehead, the three bullets a mirror image of the assassination of his brother Mick. Kieran then returned to his room, and finished packing the few items he had brought with him back into his large holdall, and waited quietly for the return of his wife.

As Kieran sat patiently in his hotel room, his wife Shelagh was knocking on the door of Declan and Jimmy

McConnell's twin room in their hotel about half a mile away. She was dressed in a smart, plain black knee-length skirt and white blouse, all purchased that afternoon and very similar to the attire of the hotel's chambermaids, and carrying several neatly folded towels, which Fergal and Ardal had supplied from their own room on the floor below. Earlier, she had been sat in the reception foyer waiting for the twins to return to their room and, on finally seeing them entering the hotel through the main front entrance and heading over to the lifts, she waited a couple of minutes before quickly going up to her two Irish colleagues' room, where they were waiting for her signal to follow her. The two men were now stood on either side of the twins' hotel room door, backs flat against the wall, both holding handguns with silencer attachments, which were hidden from view behind their backs. Shelagh, who was stood between Ardal and Fergal and straight in front of the room door, called "Room service" loudly, knocking on the door again, before looking quickly up and down the corridor, checking no other guests had suddenly appeared from the lifts or other rooms. The twins were both sat on their respective beds watching the 'News' on the large flat-screen TV, which was fixed onto a movable arm, halfway up the opposite wall. As Jimmy was on the bed nearest the door, he jumped up, looked through the small 'spy hole' which was at head height in the room's door, and seeing what appeared to be a maid carrying some towels, opened the door before saying politely in his broad 'scouse' accent, "We already have towels, thanks luv."

"Yes, I know sir," Shelagh replied, disguising her Irish accent as best she could, "but apparently the maid forgot to change yours for clean ones this morning. It won't take a minute sir, sorry for the interruption." And before Jimmy could reply Shelagh walked past him and marched into the room, heading towards the bathroom, before disappearing inside and closing the door behind herself, nodding at Declan as she went by him. Jimmy was stood inside the room, holding the door half open, looking at the 'maid' as she walked into their bathroom, when two men suddenly followed her through the door, each holding a silenced handgun, and closed the door behind themselves, taking the twins completely by surprise. The two men crossed the room quickly, standing in front of the bathroom door facing the astonished Liverpudlians. Without saying a word and before their targets had chance to speak, the two guns fired at almost the same time; four loud 'pops' were the only sounds that were made, and those were lost amongst the measured delivery of the television newscaster. The twins were both hit twice in the chest, the soft point bullets, the same type that Kieran had used on Underwood, expanding on impact, causing massive internal injuries and as was intended, remaining in the now limp bodies which slumped slowly to the floor. As previously instructed by Kieran, Fergal and Ardal laid the twins out neatly on their backs, arms by their sides and legs together, before each shooting one of the twins through the centre of their respective foreheads. They then knocked on the bathroom door and called Shelagh, who walked carefully past the two bodies, avoiding the now pooling blood and giving them both a cursory glance, before opening the room door. After checking that there was no-one in the corridor to see them leave, she led her two colleagues out, still carrying the towels, back to their room, carefully pulling the twins' room door shut behind them as they left. Shelagh then waited while they packed everything they had brought with them, including the guns which they would dispose of later, into their two backpacks. Once they had finished, Shelagh had a good look round, double checking they had not left anything behind, before she left their room and walked quickly back to her own hotel. Five minutes after Shelagh left, Ardal followed her out of the room, and then after another five minutes, he was then followed by Fergal, both carrying their backpacks casually over their shoulders. Instead of going to Kieran's hotel, as Shelagh had done, they headed straight to Euston Station, where they would meet up later with their two colleagues, before all four of them would catch the train North to Manchester. They had both paid for their rooms in advance, so the hotel management would not raise any alarms when they discovered that their guests had vacated their respective rooms early. After arriving in Manchester, they would stay overnight there, before catching an early morning train to Bangor, and then another one to Holyhead on Anglesey, before boarding the 2:10pm ferry to Dublin, and then the final leg back to Belfast by train.

It was while they were travelling on the train to Bangor that the police were first called to the two hotels in central London, alerted by the hotel management after two sets of hysterical chambermaids had discovered the three bodies during their morning rounds.

The two investigations were quickly escalated from the local police station to New Scotland Yard's Serious Crimes division, firstly because of the obvious similarity between the two separate crime scenes, but also because of the potential major diplomatic ramifications that would undoubtedly ensue when it was discovered that not only was one of the victims employed by a foreign dignitary, but that it also occurred at an hotel owned by the Dubai Royal family.

When the two new police files finally landed on the desk of Chief Superintendent Washbourne, to be opened later that afternoon on his return from a departmental meeting, Kieran O'Hare, his wife and two fellow gang members, had just boarded an Irish Ferry about to sail from Holyhead to Dublin. And when Washbourne eventually returned to his office and picked up the two files marked 'Urgent', Kieran, flanked on either side by his wife Shelagh and his two colleagues, was casually leaning over the handrail of the ferry, and dropping the three handguns and their silencer attachments into the depths of the Irish Sea.

Chapter 34

When Chief Superintendent Washbourne returned to his office later that afternoon, after chairing a departmental review with all his senior officers, he sat down at his desk and opened the two files marked 'Urgent', which had been placed there earlier in the day by his Personal Assistant.

The first one he looked at, outlined what looked like a professional execution of two brothers, named by the hotel management where they were found, as Declan and Jimmy McConnell. As soon as he read their names, he immediately opened the second report, and quickly scanned the first couple of paragraphs, until he came to the name of the third victim, given by the second hotel manager where he was found, as a solicitor called Jonathon Jones, who was on business over from Dubai.

Stunned, the Chief Superintendent read both files through twice, before picking up his desk phone and speaking to his PA, who was sat at the desk just outside his office.

"Sandra, please find Detective Inspector Greenwood wherever he is and whatever he is doing, and ask him to come to my office at his earliest convenience. Thank you," said Washbourne, and replaced the phone on its base.

Ten minutes later, his desk phone rang and the Chief Superintendent immediately picked it up and spoke, "Yes Sandra?"

"DI Greenwood will be here very shortly Sir, as fortunately he was already in the building."

"Excellent Sandra, thank you very much," said Washbourne, and replaced the receiver.

Twenty minutes after the Chief Superintendent made the initial request to his PA, there was a knock on his office door. Washbourne immediately pressed a button on the underside of his desk, by his right knee, which silently released a bolt on his office door, and the sign above the outside of the door changed from 'Engaged' to 'Enter'. The door silently swung open, and DI Greenwood entered his boss's office, closing the door behind himself and walking across the small office towards the desk. CS Washbourne looked up, and with a nod of his head, signalled Greenwood to sit down on one of the two chairs across from himself, on the other side of the desk.

"Thank you for coming so promptly, Richard," Washbourne said, picking up the two manila files he had been reading again and passing them across the desk to the Detective Inspector. "Before you read those," Washbourne continued before Greenwood had chance to open either of the folders, "where are you up to with the Underwood case?"

After a brief pause, the Detective Inspector replied, "Nothing new to report really Sir, unfortunately. We have been monitoring the emails and mobile calls of his wife Abigail and his two associates, the McConnell twins, but nothing out of the ordinary. We have also kept an eye on their bank accounts, and again, nothing suspicious. Quite honestly Sir, we are at a loss as to what more we can do;

it looks like we might have to close the enquiry. We are no nearer locating our elusive solicitor, the missing money, or the mysterious IT man. There has been no contact by anyone with Emrys Williams, Underwood's partner, while he has been in Strangeways. He is due out next year if, as we presume, he is granted parole after serving half of his sentence," DI Greenwood answered.

"As I thought," Washbourne said, before breaking into a smile and continuing, pointing at the two unopened files. "Those came in earlier today. Please have a read - they might help your investigations somewhat."

The Detective Inspector read the two files in shocked silence, before looking up at his superior officer. "Well, at least that answers the question of what happened to Underwood after he skipped the country, and how he has eluded our search for him," Greenwood spoke eventually. "But now we have a whole new enquiry, as to how he become involved with the Sheik, who has executed him and the McConnells, and why."

"Exactly Richard. It may well be that everything is interlinked, or it might be that their deaths and Underwood's new life in Dubai are completely separate. Whatever the case, as a matter of urgency, first we need to find Underwood's and the McConnells' killers. If you need more personnel, just ask and I will get it cleared."

"Will do Sir," and DI Greenwood picked up the two files and quickly left his superior's office, before returning to his own office, and sending emails to all the officers who had been involved in the search for Jonathon T Underwood and the missing millions of pounds, and arranging an urgent meeting for the following morning at 8:30am, in one of the conference rooms on the third floor of New Scotland Yard.

The meeting started promptly at the designated time, and DI Greenwood distributed copies of the two files CS Washbourne had presented to him the previous afternoon, to all the assembled officers, who had been instructed to cancel any previous appointments, and present themselves at one of the third-floor conference rooms that morning.

"Good morning gentlemen," the Detective Inspector opened the meeting, once everyone had settled down around the large oval conference table. "I have asked you all here today, because there has been a major development in the Jonathon Underwood investigation, which as you are all aware has not been going too well. Before I say any more, please read the two files in front of each of you," and Greenwood fell silent as the ten officers each opened the first file and started reading.

When all the officers had finally read both files, and looked up at their commanding officer in silent astonishment, Greenwood continued.

"At least we now know where Underwood is, and where he has been for the last couple of years. However, we now have two very new investigations to carry out. Firstly, obviously find whoever has carried out the executions of Underwood and the McConnells. The killers, and we are almost certainly looking at two different perpetrators, want us to know that they are connected, by the obvious similarities between the two executions. They are definitely a statement. The fact that they are connected, should point us to the reason why they were carried out, and by whom. It is up to us to find that connection. Secondly, we need to discover how Underwood was able to escape our initial investigations into his criminal activity, and how he set up an apparently new life in Dubai under his original family name, and who helped him. Do not expect any help from the Sheik and his people, as they will want to keep any association with the solicitor and his death as quiet as possible. We have already received a warning off from their Embassy, and our people in Whitehall, so tread very carefully." The Detective Inspector paused briefly, while his officers took in the new situation they were faced with, before continuing.

"The first task is to get as much CCTV footage from the two hotels, from the time that Underwood and the McConnells checked in, till a day after the murders, and interview the various members of staff, and check out all the guests registered at the time in the hotels, and any visitors who might appear in the CCTV footage. See if they met or talked to anyone during their stays. We need to know what the three of them were doing together in London. We know Underwood, under his new name of Jones, was here on legitimate business with the Sheik, but it cannot be coincidence the three of them were here at the same time. Interview anyone who they spoke to or met. Again, I must stress, that when dealing with the Sheik's hotel staff and guests, tread softly. They may not be overly forthcoming with their CCTV, because of who might have been staying there, but get what you can. If you need extra staff, let me know. I cannot emphasise the importance of this new investigation, both in helping us close the Underwood case successfully at last, but also bringing the perpetrators of three callous executions to justice. I have split you into two teams, your individual assignment and team leader is printed on the front of each file. I want daily reports, and to be informed immediately of any major development. Thank you, gentlemen."

As DI Greenwood was bringing his meeting to a close, Kieran and Shelagh O'Hare were boarding a Ryanair flight to Malaga, and their two compatriots Fergal and Ardal were already in the air, on an earlier EasyJet flight to the same destination. All four were flying under different names, aliases set up many years before, in order for the gang members to live anonymously in Spain, away from any possible police investigations, if required. The O'Hares had owned the villa in Marbella for over twelve years now, the ultimate destination of the four Northern Ireland citizens, under their aliases, and all four held dual nationality, both British and Spanish.

Chapter 35

The team conducting the investigation into the McConnell twins' deaths, as expected, were receiving the full co-operation of their hotel's management and the security staff. They were supplied immediately on request with a copy of all the CCTV footage from inside the hotel for the entire duration of the twins' stay, plus a list of all the guests staying there at the time and their contact details. The hotel also provided similarly comprehensive details for all their staff.

Half of the team concentrated their efforts on examining the large amount of CCTV footage, drafting in an extra two personnel from a separate department to help speed up the process, while the other three members worked on the guest and hotel staff lists.

The second team, looking into the Jones/Underwood execution, also as expected, were not so fortunate regarding co-operation from the solicitor's hotel. They received an abridged list of the hotel's guests and staff, which excluded everyone associated either directly or indirectly with royal citizens of Dubai and their personal staff, later on the afternoon of the commencement of the investigation. But it was not until the following morning, that the team received a very heavily censored copy of the CCTV footage from the hotel's security system. It was accompanied by an assurance from the hotel's Head of Security, that the few discs contained all the footage in which the deceased, Jonathon Jones, appeared, and everyone that the solicitor had met within the hotel during his stay. The short accompanying report also contained a copy of Jones's official appointments, which he had carried out on behalf of the Sheik during their visit to London. The footage included, as the team eventually discovered after examining the edited footage, Jones meeting up with someone in reception, before going into the Grosvenor bar with him for a short meeting. On questioning the young lady on reception at the time, she remembered that the man had a strong South African accent, and that he did not have an appointment to see Mr Jones, but that Mr Jones, when informed of his presence, was happy to come down from his room to see him. What the investigating team did not know, was that the South African gentleman in question was quickly identified by the Sheik's Head of Security, who had been editing the CCTV footage before its delivery to the police, as Andre Botha, who was very well known to the Sheik and his Head of Security, as the South African had been employed by them both for several years previously. When it also came to light that it was Botha who had recommended Jones to the Sheik's legal department, alarm bells were ringing within the Sheik's staff, which resulted in a hastily arranged 'Zoom' meeting between the Sheik, his Head of Security, and the head of his Legal Department back in Dubai. The meeting was short, and resulted in the decision to remove the link between the Sheik and the execution, and the threat of any possible embarrassing situation arising from it. The Head of Security, together with one of his team, were immediately sent to Botha's head office. On their arrival there, Botha having been informed who his unexpected guests were, the two security men were shown straight through to the South African's office. After a short discussion, during which to Andre's astonishment he was told of the violent death of Jonathon Jones, and was also informed that under no circumstances was he to be allowed to be interviewed by the police, a directive the South African readily agreed to, the three men then re-emerged together from the office again. As he left his office shortly afterwards, accompanied by his two unexpected guests, Botha informed his secretary that he would be out for the rest of the day, and for her to cancel the two appointments he had later in the afternoon. From there, the South African was driven directly to a private airport South of London, one he had used himself many times when in the employ of the Sheik, where he boarded a private jet enroute to Dubai, landing there sixteen hours before the police received the CCTV footage from Jones's/Underwood's hotel.

When the CCTV footage finally arrived at New Scotland Yard, along with the edited guest list, it did not take the detectives long to identify Underwood's visitors to his hotel. Firstly, there was his meeting with the South African, who was identified as Andre Botha the following day. Unfortunately for the police, who were very keen to interview him, Botha was by then safely hidden away in a bungalow on the Sheik's estate in Dubai, where he would shortly be re-employed on the Sheik's personal protection detail, never to return to the UK again. Secondly, his meeting with the McConnell brothers, the evening before Botha turned up at the hotel, was also identified and logged.

Then, from the two hotel guests' lists, it was quickly noted that two guests from each hotel checked out early from their respective rooms, on the evening of the murders and before the three bodies were discovered the following morning. In addition, both rooms, a double occupied by a man and a woman and a twin occupied by two men, had coincidentally been paid for in full in advance, so no alarms had been raised when they had left early without checking out. On looking back through the CCTV footage from both hotels, the two sets of guests were seen leaving their hotels separately. It was also picked up that the woman from Underwood's hotel was seen entering the McConnells' hotel earlier that same evening, and leaving it again just over an hour later, shortly before the two men left. At no time, during any of the footage from the two hotels, did the four guests appear to meet up. Unfortunately for the police, when the two men from the McConnells' hotel first arrived and met up with O'Hare at his hotel, although it was captured on CCTV, as Underwood did not appear on any of that footage and they were not people of interest at the time, it was not included in the edited package that was delivered by the hotel security manager to the investigating officers.

When the staff from both hotels were initially questioned about the four guests, no one had any recollection of them, or remembered anything about them. When the police tried to trace them from the information the hotel held for them, they soon discovered that they had used false names and addresses, and the credit cards used to pay for both the rooms were stolen. However, the day after being questioned by one of the police officers, one of the staff serving behind the Grosvenor bar called the same officer back, on the number the detective had given him. The barman told the officer that he had just been watching the BBC news, when a man from Belfast was being interviewed, and when the man spoke in his broad Belfast accent, it immediately reminded him of a conversation he had had, with a man he had served on one of the evenings he had been quizzed about, and he thought that the man may have been one of the people the police had asked him about.

This new information was quickly relayed via the team leader to DI Greenwood, who knowing Underwood's previous links to Belfast and the murders out at Larne, immediately understood the potential importance of this development.

Within an hour of the barman reporting his latest recollections to the police detective, coupled with the suspicious early checkout of the four guests, copies of screenshots, taken from the CCTV from the two hotels of the four 'people of interest', were being emailed from DI Greenwood, Serious Crimes Division, New Scotland Yard, to his opposite number at the Northern Ireland Police Headquarters on Knock Road, Belfast, marked 'Urgent' and with a request for any information regarding the enclosed.

Within an hour, Greenwood received a short, but very informative, reply which read, "The first man and woman are Kieran and Shelagh O'Hare. Kieran is the head of a very well-known criminal organisation in Belfast, and Shelagh is his wife. The other two men are Fergal Donovan and Ardal Finnegan, and are known 'enforcers' for O'Hare's organisation. We have very comprehensive files on all four. Let me know if you require anything further."

Greenwood immediately replied, "They are people of interest to us, in a suspected execution of three people over here in London very recently. Please could you detain the four of them as quickly as possible for questioning. You can reach me on the number at the bottom of this email with any developments. Regards, Richard Greenwood.

PS: Were Mick and Aileen O'Hare, who were discovered buried at the farm in Larne, related to Kieran?"

Again, the reply was immediate, "Yes, he was Kieran's brother. Is there a connection to your investigation?"

"Yes indeed. I will let you have the full details shortly," and with that, the two police officers ended their communication for the time being.

After re-reading the emails from Belfast, Greenwood smiled and spoke aloud to himself, "Well, we know who killed them and why; obviously revenge for his brother's death and, as we correctly suspected, Underwood and the McConnells were involved. Now it is up to our colleagues in Belfast to find them for us."

Following his conversation with Belfast, Greenwood put a call through to Chief Superintendent Washbourne, informing him of the breakthrough in their investigations into the three deaths in London, before calling a meeting of all the officers involved in their investigation, for the following morning at New Scotland Yard.

Chapter 36

Brian Connolly arrived in Inverness two days after leaving Newcastle, having taken a circuitous route across Scotland via Kilmarnock, Oban and Fort William, enjoying the fabulous views on the way, before booking into a local hotel. He unpacked his small holdall with the few things he had brought in from the campervan, and then booted up his laptop to see if there was anything interesting happening in the world, or at least London anyway. He had spent the previous night in a layby on the outskirts of Largs on the West coast, where there was no internet or cellular connection, and had remained blissfully unaware of what was happening back in England's capital.

Once the laptop 'booted up', Connolly connected it to the internet, using his iPhone's 4G Wi-Fi service as an internet 'hotspot', not trusting the hotel's own public wi-fi facility. Then clicking on his mail 'inbox', he immediately saw that the last received message was from his friend and colleague, ex-Captain Cunningham. The message was short, but exactly what he had hoped it to be, although he was a little surprised that it had been sent so soon after he had left London.

The message read, "Please contact me ASAP. Jones and those two men/brothers? who he met in his hotel, and you asked me to keep an eye on, have been found dead this morning in their hotel rooms. TC"

Connolly read the short message for a second time, before letting out a large sigh of relief; his speculative plans had born fruit sooner than he could have dreamed of. Hopefully, this would mean that he was reasonably safe, at least from his ex-criminal associates. Now he would have to wait and see if there was any fallout from the police investigation, which could result in him being implicated in some way, although he was pretty sure that although they knew of his existence, he was confident that they had no idea as to his actual identity.

He also knew that he would very shortly have to deal with a certain very dangerous South African who, although he might suspect that Connolly was in some way connected to his recently deceased associate's death, he was hoping would agree to continue to keep each other's past criminal association between themselves.

To that end, the ex-Intelligence Corps serviceman switched on the PAYG phone, the number of which was his main point of contact between himself and the South African. He was not surprised, having received the message from Tony Cunningham, when as soon as the phone went live, the phone 'pinged' and the 'message received' icon appeared on the display screen. He tapped on the icon and the message was instantly displayed. Again, it was short and to the point and it read "Please contact ASAP. We need to speak. AB".

Connolly firstly replied to his ex-serviceman colleague's email message. "Am out of the country at the moment, will call you immediately on my return. Please keep me informed of any new developments. Regards BC."

He took a little more time with his reply to Andre Botha. He needed to stall the South African for as long as possible while the initial police investigation developed, as he wanted to stay well away from any possible involvement. He knew it would not take the team at New Scotland Yard long to uncover the three bodies' true identities, and the flurry of activity on their part once they discovered that one of the dead men was Jonathon T Underwood, travelling under the name of Jones and recently arrived from Dubai, where he was residing and had been since his disappearance a few years ago. With their new information, albeit posthumously in the case of Underwood and the McConnell twins, the police would undoubtedly uncover possible links from Underwood to Andre Botha, and guess to his own involvement in their past history, albeit anonymously in his case. He felt safer, both from Botha and the police where he was, innocently touring the Highlands of Scotland.

Instead of replying to the South African's text, Connolly sent a message to Botha's office email address, which read, "Am currently out of the country with little to no cellular coverage. I will contact you as soon as I return in a couple of weeks' time. Please use this secure email address if you require me urgently. Can confirm you have no concerns regarding our relationship." Connolly knew that there was a good chance the email would possibly be read by the police if, as he presumed, Botha would be investigated once his connection to Jones/Underwood was established, the South African being instrumental in getting the solicitor the job with his new employer in Dubai. But the message's origin and content, intentionally suitably vague, would be impossible to trace back to him, and was no way incriminating to either party. The ex-Int Corps man stayed on line, hoping for a quick response and he was rewarded when, twenty minutes later, a new message appeared in his 'inbox', having been routed via many different servers in a corresponding number of different countries. It was from Botha, equally vague, and from a different anonymous email address, and read, "Understood. Am not disappointed with latest developments. Share your views on our relationship." What Connolly did not know was that his emails had been picked up remotely and replied to from a laptop in a bungalow in Dubai, and that the South African no longer posed any threat to himself.

When Connolly read Botha's reply, he was mightily relieved, and not a little puzzled, by the South African's apparent acceptance, not to say possible pleasure, of Underwood's death, and he wondered what might have gone on between the two of them. Whatever it was, Connolly thought, he was very pleased with it, and felt much more positive about his own survival prospects, both from the South African and also possible capture by the police, as Botha was now the only person who knew his true identity, and who was linked to his criminal past.

The ex-Int Corps serviceman then spent a short time searching through the BBC News website, for anything to do with the deaths of Underwood/Jones and the McConnells, but there was little about either killing, which surprised him a little at first. However, on reflection, he presumed that as Underwood was employed by a foreign dignitary, and the execution took place in one of their family's hotels, they would be keeping it as low key in the media as possible, probably on a strongly worded request from the Emirates' Embassy. There was a brief mention of the McConnells' deaths in their hotel, but there were no details, and it was not linked in the article to Underwood's identical execution half a mile away.

After gleaning as much information as he could about the two incidents from various other news websites, Connolly closed his laptop and went downstairs to the hotel's small restaurant for his evening meal, having decided to enjoy an extended holiday exploring the wilderness territories of Northern Scotland.

Chapter 37

The meeting in a different, smaller third-floor conference room, for all the officers involved in the Underwood and McConnell shootings, started promptly at 8:30am. DI Greenwood was sat at the head of the large oblong table, with the officers spread evenly around the other three sides, their personal action files on the desk in front of each one.

After calling the meeting to order, the Detective Inspector addressed the assembled police officers.

"Last evening, we had, what I firmly believe, was a major breakthrough in our enquiries into the deaths of Underwood and the McConnell brothers," Greenwood announced, pausing briefly for effect, before continuing. "We are confident that we have identified the people involved in both shootings."

There was a collective intake of breath from the investigating officers, who were unaware of this major development, and were all just expecting a regular update of the case so far. The policemen noticeably sat up and were now looking, fully focused, at their commanding officer.

"We believe that there were four people involved," Greenwood continued, looking at each of his officers in turn as he spoke. "They are Kieran and Shelagh O'Hare, and two of their associates, Fergal Donovan and Ardal Finnegan. They are from Northern Ireland, and their identities have been confirmed by our colleagues over in Belfast. Kieran O'Hare, we have also been informed, is the head of a very well-known, non-political criminal organisation based in Belfast, and is the brother of Mick O'Hare who, as most of you will know, was shot along with his wife Aileen, and a colleague Jerry Duggan, several years ago at Mick's farmhouse in Larne, just outside Belfast. At the time of those shootings, we suspected that they were in some way connected to, what we believed but was never proven, Jonathon Underwood's alleged gemstone smuggling operation, based on Anglesey in North Wales. Again, we were unable to prove Underwood's involvement in the gemstone smuggling, although we did eventually obtain convictions for his associate Emrys Williams, and of course our notorious ex-Chief Superintendent, now also deceased, Jonny Radcliffe. Our four new suspects were checked into the two hotels at the time when the shootings took place, and all four left their respective hotels later the same evening as the murders. So, they had opportunity and certainly motive, that being revenge for the killing of Kieran's brother and sister-in-law and their associate Jerry Duggan. We have already put all the airports and ferry terminals on alert for the four, but they have a good forty-eight hours start on us, and are probably already back in Northern Ireland, or maybe even further afield. Again, our colleagues in Belfast are helping with an intensive search for the four of them over there, and will notify us immediately if they have any news. In the meantime, we need to concentrate all our efforts in finding everything we can about the four suspects' movements since they arrived in London, where they went, if they met anyone while they were here, anything that will help us put together a comprehensive picture of their activities prior to, and after, the shootings. We also need to redouble our searches of the two crime scenes, in the hope of finding some forensic evidence that places whoever did the actual shootings, at the scene of each crime. When we find these four people, and I am confident that we will, we need to be able to charge them with more than just using false identities, and paying their room bills with stolen credit cards." Greenwood paused again before continuing. "We also need to redouble our efforts to find, and interview, the South African, Andre Botha. Although we now believe he was not involved with the shootings, I would still like to question him regarding his relationship with Underwood, and how he was involved with our elusive solicitor. We know Botha had ties with Dubai, both before he moved his business here to London, and since, and it may well have been the South African who helped set up Underwood with his new life over there in Dubai."

After asking for any questions from the assembled police detectives, of which there were none, the Detective Inspector closed the meeting and the officers returned to their newly refined searches, with a definite feeling of optimism and a spring in their step.

Chapter 38

While Detective Inspector Greenwood's team of police officers, together with help from their colleagues in Northern Ireland, were still diligently searching for Andre Botha, and their four chief suspects in the shootings of Jonathon T Underwood and the McConnell brothers, Brian Connelly, whilst enjoying his extended touring holiday in the Highlands of Scotland, was conducting his own unsuccessful search for Andre Botha. It was triggered after he received a second message from his friend and fellow ex-serviceman, Tony Cunningham, which informed him that the police so far seemed to have made no progress in apprehending the killers of Underwood and the McConnells, and the South African seemed to have disappeared completely. Cunningham had made several enquiries as to Botha's whereabouts, within his network of private investigator contacts, both personally and by his own company operatives, but without any success.

Connolly had sent the South African several further emails to, what he presumed was a secure email address, the one Botha had used when he last contacted the ex-Int Corps man, none of which elicited any reply from Botha. Eventually, three weeks after the three murders, Connolly finally decided to return to London, feeling confident that whatever the police had discovered about the executions and who might be involved, he certainly was not included in any of their investigations. Regular checking on his laptop of the CCTV camera footage and the various alarm systems in his homes, showed there had been no visits to any of the three residences, either during the day by the official forces of law and order, or nocturnally, very unofficially, by anyone else.

He arrived firstly at his Newcastle house late in the afternoon, after driving down in the campervan from Aberdeen, where he had spent the previous night, after returning on the ferry from a week in Kirkwall in the Orkney Islands, somewhere he had always wanted to visit. He returned all his camping gear and waterproof, outdoor clothing and walking boots back into storage in the attic of the house, before driving the campervan round to a fellow Newcastle United supporter's car repair and MOT business, where his friend had offered to garage the vehicle for him until he might need it again. Connolly thanked his friend once again for the use of his garage, and gave him a very generous thousand pounds in used twenty pounds notes for his trouble, which at first the garage owner refused to take, but was eventually persuaded to do so, and promised his fellow 'Toon' fanatic, that he would be back up for Newcastle's first home game of the new season.

Connolly then returned to his house by taxi, and the following morning packed what he needed to take back to London and called for another taxi, which arrived promptly thirty minutes later to take him to the main station, and a train back to England's capital city.

On arriving back at his London flat, the ex-Int Corps man dropped off his case, and the backpack which contained his laptop and accessories, and went straight over to the

Veterans' Centre in Lewisham, where he had earlier arranged to meet ex-Captain Cunningham, asking him to bring along the two packages he had left with him for safe keeping, and the return of the said packages to himself, which he would later destroy, no longer having a need for either. He also asked Tony for an update regarding the police investigation into the three executions and the search for Andre Botha. When Cunningham informed him at their meeting that there was nothing new to report on either matter, and that Botha was still missing, Connolly finally relaxed, and breathed a large sigh of relief as he left the Centre to return to his flat. Botha was the only person left who knew Connolly's identity, and it looked like he was either also now deceased, on whose orders he could hazard a very good guess, or more probably, that the same Middle Eastern dignitary, fearing the inevitable diplomatic fallout if Botha's links to him and Underwood came to light, had had Botha removed to somewhere where the English police authorities would not be able to find him. Either way, Connolly was convinced he was now completely in the clear, and could happily live the rest of his life quietly, wherever he wanted to, and doing whatever he wanted to, complete with a very healthy bank balance.

Chapter 39

It was just over four weeks after Jonathon Underwood and the McConnell brothers had been professionally executed, that Detective Inspector Greenwood was sat across the desk in front of his commanding officer, Chief Superintendent Washbourne, at New Scotland Yard.

After the initial pleasantries, Washbourne brought the conversation round to the reason for their meeting.

"Well Richard, what do you have for me?" he asked the Detective Inspector, more in hope than expectation, looking at the expression on his face.

Without referring to the rather large, unopened manila file on the desk in front of himself, Greenwood replied, after a short pause.

"So far Sir, I am afraid we have drawn a complete blank," the deflated Detective Inspector replied. "Our main suspects from across the Irish Sea seemed to have completely disappeared, and our colleagues over in Belfast have been unable to find any trace whatsoever of the four of them since the shootings. The forensic teams, again, have found nothing which could help us to put any of the four at either crime scene, neither have we found the guns which fired the nine bullets, which were all still lodged in the three bodies. We have similarly been unable to trace the South African, Andre Botha, who, although we don't believe was involved in the shootings, we are obviously very keen to interview regarding his past association with Jonathon Underwood, and his and the solicitor's previous possible criminal activities. We have never been able to prove anything against Underwood, or find the mysterious IT man, who we believe was able to hide the many millions of pounds that went missing, when we arrested the accountant Williams and our ex-Chief Superintendent Jonny Radcliffe. Now that Underwood has gone, we are pretty sure that Botha is probably our last potential link towards the solicitor's past criminal activities, the lost monies and the identity of the IT man. All we do know about Botha was that the morning after the shootings, two well-dressed men of, what the receptionist at the South African's office believes, were perhaps of middle eastern appearance, arrived at the office without an appointment, to see Botha. Having been informed of their presence, Botha immediately asked the receptionist to show them both through to him. Shortly afterwards, the South African, accompanied by the two men, reappeared from his office. Botha, who again according to the receptionist, seemed calm and relaxed, asked his secretary to cancel the two appointments he had for later in the day, before leaving the office with his two guests. Since that time, no-one has seen or heard from the South African again."

"It would seem that Jonathon Underwood is proving as much a thorn in our side dead, as he was when he was alive, Richard," Washbourne commented when the Detective Inspector had finished his report. "I presume you think the two mysterious middle eastern gentlemen are something to do with the Sheik, which again, I presume has been denied by his office?"

"Exactly Sir, right on both assumptions. Unfortunately, unless Botha miraculously reappears sometime in the future, I think we are unlikely to see him again, and certainly not in London. I think it is considered that he could present a potential diplomatic embarrassment in certain Dubai-based circles, so they have removed the threat. However, we are still hopeful that we will eventually be able to lay our hands on Kieran and Shelagh O'Hare and their two colleagues; they cannot stay in hiding indefinitely, but so far, we are not able to place any of them at either crime scene. We will of course keep trying to turn something up, but the forensic teams have gone over both rooms twice without any luck, so unfortunately, I have to admit it is doubtful we would be able to secure any convictions with what we have so far, Sir," Greenwood admitted to the Chief Superintendent. "However, on a slightly more positive note, we do have another possible future line of enquiry," the Detective Inspector continued before Washbourne could pass any comment, "albeit a bit of a longshot. The only other link we have to Underwood's past, the accountant Emrys Williams, is up for parole later next year, which I am sure will be granted. It was Williams who told us about the IT man's existence during his evidence at his trial, but unfortunately, apart from a reasonably vague physical description of the man, could not provide any more information about his identity, who he was or where he lived at the time. If, and when, Williams is released, we will of course keep a very close eye on him; what he does, where he goes, and if he suddenly seems to acquire a large sum of money or any other notable possessions, from wherever, either here in the UK, or possibly from abroad. Unfortunately for us, one of Williams's main attributes within their criminal organisation, was the ability to transfer large amounts of cash invisibly around the world through various offshore bank accounts, so keeping tabs on his financial situation will not be very straightforward. Our hope is that Williams might lead us eventually to either the IT man, and hence the missing millions, or possibly even Botha," the Detective Inspector suggested, but without much conviction.

"All in all, once again, concerning Jonathon T Underwood, not our finest hour Richard," the Chief Superintendent concluded after a brief pause.

"No Sir, definitely not," the Detective Inspector agreed.

LOOSE ENDS

Epilogue

Ten months after the death of Jonathon T Underwood, Emrys Williams was released from Strangeways Prison, having been successfully paroled after serving half of his eight year prison sentence. Three weeks after his release, he received an official looking envelope by recorded delivery, with a Dubai postmark, in the post at his rented flat in Didsbury, Manchester. The envelope was from a Dubai-based solicitor's office and contained a first-class, one-way flight to Dubai for two weeks on Thursday, a booking confirmation for a double room at a prestigious hotel in central Dubai, and a letter from the solicitors inviting him to the reading of the Final Will and Testament of Jonathon T Jones. It also requested that he confirm his attendance for the reading as soon as possible, either by telephone or email as below. An identical letter and contents were also delivered, again by recorded delivery, to Jonathon's ex-wife, now widow, at her Alderley Edge apartment.

On opening the letter and reading it through, Emrys immediately emailed confirmation of his intended attendance on the stated date, back to the Dubai solicitor's office.

Abigail did not reply until the following day, but after careful consideration regarding any possible criminal implications, and satisfying herself that there would be no repercussions, and never having visited Dubai before, she also emailed her intention to attend the solicitor's Dubai office in two weeks' time.

Abigail and Emrys were booked on different flights and into separate hotels, so arrived at the solicitor's office on the second floor of their Dubai downtown offices without meeting, and with no knowledge of the other person's requested attendance at the reading of the will. Emrys was the first to arrive, ten minutes before the appointed time of 10am, the day after arriving in Dubai. After identifying himself to the receptionist, he was shown through to a large conference room, just off the open plan reception area, where there was a large jug of iced water and a heated coffee jug, cups and glasses on a side table, alongside another table with a plate of pastries and biscuits. Abigail arrived five minutes later, and was also shown through to the same room by the young receptionist, who introduced the two visitors to each other, the pair surprisingly never having met before throughout the accountant's long association with her now deceased husband, before leaving them alone together, after inviting them both to help themselves to any refreshments. As they both approached the coffee table, Emrys signalled for Abigail to get her cup first, before following her to the table and filling his own cup. Neither selected anything from the other plates, before sitting down on opposite sides of the conference table in silence. Emrys initially made an effort to engage Abigail in small talk, but they soon lapsed into another uneasy silence, as Abigail's responses were almost totally monosyllabic, and she showed no signs of wanting to enter into any conversation with, who she knew, was her ex-husband's partner in crime. Fortunately for the both of them breaking the awkward silence, a tall, very professionally dressed woman in a black knee-length skirt, matching black jacket and shoes, and a pristine white blouse, and carrying a blue file, followed by an equally professionally attired young man, entered the conference room five minutes later and walked first to Abigail and shook her hand firmly. She then did the same with Emrys, before introducing herself, in what sounded like a faint American accent, as Sandy Kingham, a senior partner in the Dubai law firm, and pointing to her colleague, announced him as Peter, a junior paralegal, who was carrying a small notepad and pen.

Sandy briskly thanked them for making the long journey to Dubai, before sitting down at the head of the table, Peter next to her on her left ready to take notes as required, and indicating to Abigail and Emrys to sit back down on her right.

The solicitor then opened the blue file, and took out two sheets of white A4 paper, placing them separately on the table in front of her, before looking up and speaking to the two expectant visitors.

"Before I read Jonathan's will, or at least the parts that apply to each of you, please let me reassure you both that we have made extensive enquiries into the legitimacy of this document, in the light of how he met his death last year, and the subsequent police investigation, surrounding any possible criminal activity he may or may not have been involved in." The solicitor looked from

Abigail to Emrys in turn as she spoke, with her gaze resting on the former accountant as she alluded to the criminal activity. She paused slightly and then continued. "Jonathon Jones was a legally registered citizen and solicitor in Dubai, carrying out legitimate legal services of behalf of a local dignitary here in the city, and following the investigations of New Scotland Yard last year after his sudden violent death, no charges were brought against him posthumously, either in the UK or here in Dubai. This means that Mr Jones has no criminal record, again either in the UK, here, or anywhere else in the world. This also means that any monies, real estate or other possessions held in his name here in Dubai, that he has bequeathed in his legally attested will, can in any way be contested, or subject to future scrutiny by any official authorities, again either here in Dubai or back in the UK. In fact, Mr Jones was at great pains to point this out to us, himself being a very accomplished solicitor as we all know, when he instructed us to write his will." Again the solicitor paused, giving Emrys and Abigail time to take in the assurances they were being given. When neither of her two visitors spoke, the solicitor continued.

"If you have no questions, I will continue and read the parts of Jonathon's will which appertain to each of you," the solicitor said, looking at both of them, as they shook their heads in silent agreement. Then picking up one of the sheets of A4 paper, she spoke firstly looking at Emrys, "To my good friend and colleague, I leave five million pounds in trust, the details of which I have provided to my solicitors, to be used, invested, or transferred howsoever he sees fit. I also strongly advise my good friend, to consult with my solicitors regarding his future, following a discussion I have had with them." Again the solicitor paused, before looking up and speaking to the ex-accountant again. "Mr Williams, if you would like to follow Paul, he will take you through to my office. I will come through to you, to pass on Mr Jones's advice, as soon as I have finished with Mrs Underwood."

At which, both Emrys and the paralegal stood up, and Emrys followed Paul out of the conference room.

When they had both left, the solicitor looked at Abigail and asked, "Before I start, do you have any questions Mrs Underwood? By the way should I call you Underwood or Jones?"

"Well actually, I have reverted back to my maiden name now of Russell, but Underwood will be fine, or Abigail, I am happy with either. And yes, I have several, but they will wait until after you read whatever is on the sheet of paper in front of you," Abigail replied nervously.

"I understand," the solicitor said, before continuing with the second part of Jonathon's final wishes. "Your husband was a very wealthy man, and how he came by that wealth, although perhaps always remaining questionable in certain official circles, will never be the subject of any future investigation here in Dubai, I can assure you."

"Thank you for that; that was one, if not the most important, question I was going to ask you," Abigail confirmed, feeling a lot better for the assurance.

"Your bequest is in two parts," the solicitor began again. "The first is a trust similar to the one for Mr Williams, in the sum of five million pounds. Again, we are instructed to administer the monies in whatever way you deem fit. We can pay regular sums into any account you nominate, or transfer the whole amount to any bank account of your choice. The second part of the bequest, is a real estate portfolio consisting of six properties, all owned in your name, within the Dubai City area, with a total present market value of just in excess of ten million pounds. There is also an additional account set up of just over two million pounds, which is used to service the properties, and again all under our control." The solicitor paused, waiting for Abigail's reaction.

"What are the properties?" was Abigail's first question, after recovering from the shock at the amount of money her ex-husband had left to her.

"There is a beach-front penthouse apartment in a very prestigious development, and the other five properties are offices in three different buildings, again in prestigious central locations, and all currently producing a very healthy rental return. We will supply you a full, up to date set of accounts, whenever you require them," the solicitor informed her.

"Okay, that's a lot to take in," she replied, again after a short pause. "Please can you give me a copy of everything, and I'll go back to my hotel, which by the way is very nice thank you, and decide what I want to do next, if that's alright with you?" Abigail asked, her mind a whirl with everything she had been told.

"Absolutely Abigail, take your time. We have the name of a very reputable financial consultant we would be happy to recommend here in Dubai, and I strongly suggest you allow us to make an appointment for you with him, before you make any decisions."

"Yes, that would be perfect, please do," Abigail replied, happy to accept the solicitor's offer.

"Right, if you go through to reception Mrs Underwood, I will get Paul to bring you a copy of all the documentation and the office accounts, and then he will call a taxi to take you back to your hotel. Take all the time you want, and I will let you know the earliest time the financial consultant can see you," and with that, the solicitor escorted Abigail out to the reception area where Paul was stood, holding another bright blue folder, before wishing her 'Goodbye' and then returning to her own office, where Emrys was patiently sat awaiting for her.

When the solicitor had settled herself back behind her desk, with Emrys sitting directly across from herself, it was Emrys who spoke first.

"What advice did Jonathon leave for me, Ms Kingham?" he asked quickly, wondering what suggestions his good friend and business associate had left for him before his untimely death.

"Before I answer that question, what are your thoughts as to what you intend to do next?" she answered.

"Obviously, unlike Abigail and my departed colleague, I do have a criminal record back in the UK, and I presume the authorities will be keeping a close eye on me and my financial accounts, and any other notable possessions that might come into my possession over the coming months. They will be acutely aware of all the money acquired by

Jonathon over his alleged, but never proven, criminal career, very little of which has ever been recovered, I understand. I am convinced I have no future back in the UK once again, as happened when I moved briefly to the States. So presently, now I have come into a little money shall we say, I am considering my options," and Emrys paused, waiting for the solicitor to reply.

After a brief silence the Dubai solicitor spoke again. "That is pretty much what Jonathon suggested would be your position, when we drew up his will. Having lived here himself for the last few years, he thinks it would be an ideal place for you to settle and start over again. He gave me a glowing reference as to your abilities as an accountant, especially your extensive expertise in the area of international money transfers, and everything that is involved in keeping said transactions as confidential and untraceable from any enquiring authorities as is possible. It is a service, all legitimate transactions only of course, we would be very interested in acquiring within our own financial team, on behalf of some of our wealthier clients, which I am proud to say is quite a long list. You would have to adopt Dubai citizenship of course, but that is something we could help with and smooth the path for you to attain. What do you say, Emrys?"

"I think it is an opportunity I would be very foolish to decline, so yes, I would certainly be open to such an offer," Emrys replied, with a broad smile on his face.

"Excellent, in that case I am sure we will be able to come to a mutually acceptable agreement. Although perhaps a little prematurely, may I welcome you to the firm Emrys, and please call me Sandy."

ABOUT THE AUTHOR

I am married to Jan, my wife of 36 years, and have two sons, Andrew 33, and Mathew 32.

I was born in Hyde, Tameside (formerly Cheshire), 71 years ago and went to St George's infants and primary school and then on to Hyde County Grammar School. I spent most of my working life as a Sales and Marketing professional and fully retired four years ago and moved down to live on the Island of Anglesey one year later with Jan from our home in Lancashire. This is my third novel and is the final chapter in 'The Anglesey Mysteries Trilogy'.

July 2023

LOOSE ENDS

Printed in Great Britain
by Amazon

24680953R00129